Praise for
Carlton Mellick III

"Easily the craziest, weirdest, strangest, funniest, most obscene writer in America."
—*GOTHIC MAGAZINE*

"Carlton Mellick III has the craziest book titles... and the kinkiest fans!"
—CHRISTOPHER MOORE, author of *The Stupidest Angel*

"If you haven't read Mellick you're not nearly perverse enough for the twenty first century."
—JACK KETCHUM, author of *The Girl Next Door*

"Carlton Mellick III is one of bizarro fiction's most talented practitioners, a virtuoso of the surreal, science fictional tale."
—CORY DOCTOROW, author of *Little Brother*

"Bizarre, twisted, and emotionally raw—Carlton Mellick's fiction is the literary equivalent of putting your brain in a blender"
—BRIAN KEENE, author of *The Rising*

"Carlton Mellick III exemplifies the intelligence and wit that lurks between its lurid covers. In a genre where crude titles are an art in themselves, Mellick is a true artist."
—*THE GUARDIAN*

"Just as Pop had Andy Warhol and Dada Tristan Tzara, the bizarro movement has its very own P. T. Barnum-type practitioner. He's the mutton-chopped author of such books as *Electric Jesus Corpse* and *The Menstruating Mall*, the illustrator, editor, and instructor of all things bizarro, and his name is Carlton Mellick III."
—*DETAILS MAGAZINE*

Also by Carlton Mellick III

Satan Burger
Electric Jesus Corpse
Sunset With a Beard (stories)
Razor Wire Pubic Hair
Teeth and Tongue Landscape
The Steel Breakfast Era
The Baby Jesus Butt Plug
Fishy-fleshed
The Menstruating Mall
Ocean of Lard (with Kevin L. Donihe)
Punk Land
Sex and Death in Television Town
Sea of the Patchwork Cats
The Haunted Vagina
Cancer-cute (Avant Punk Army Exclusive)
War Slut
Sausagey Santa
Ugly Heaven
Adolf in Wonderland
Ultra Fuckers
Cybernetrix
The Egg Man
Apeshit
The Faggiest Vampire
The Cannibals of Candyland
Warrior Wolf Women of the Wasteland
The Kobold Wizard's Dildo of Enlightenment +2
Zombies and Shit
Crab Town
The Morbidly Obese Ninja
Barbarian Beast Bitches of the Badlands
Fantastic Orgy (stories)
I Knocked Up Satan's Daughter
Armadillo Fists
The Handsome Squirm
Tumor Fruit
Kill Ball
Cuddly Holocaust

HAMMER WIVES

CARLTON MELLICK III

ERASERHEAD PRESS
PORTLAND, OREGON

ERASERHEAD PRESS
205 NE BRYANT
PORTLAND, OR 97211

WWW.ERASERHEADPRESS.COM

ISBN: 1-62105-073-4

Printed in the USA.

CONTENTS

SIMPLE MACHINES

Oliver Madu awoke one morning to discover two tiny copper doorknobs growing from the corners of his eyes. He didn't remember ever having doorknobs in his eyes before. He was pretty sure that there used to be two tiny balls of pink flesh in those parts of his eyes. They certainly weren't made of copper.

His eyes had been bothering him all through the previous day. They started out a bit itchy. Then, around lunchtime, they had turned bright red. By the time he went to sleep that night, Oliver's eyes had become swollen and throbbing. He had thought he was coming down with a flu. He hadn't realized he was growing doorknobs.

Oliver examined one of the knobs in the mirror. He tried to grab it with his thumb and index finger, but it was too tiny for his fingers to get a good grip. He tried to rub them out like morning eye-boogers, but the knobs would not budge.

Oliver decided he would attempt to ignore the knobs so that he could focus on more important things, such as getting ready for work. But as he tied his chocolate brown tie and buttoned up his beige suit, he found his attention drifting in the direction of the balls of copper.

He paused and examined the doorknobs again. He wanted to make sure they matched his work clothes. Oliver stared at his mirror image, stroking his brown business-friendly beard.

One of the doorknobs wiggled, tickling his eyelashes. Oliver moved in for a closer look.

The knob wiggled again.

He blinked two times.

Then his eyeball opened up like a door.

Behind his eyeball, there was a little man standing in the

7

open socket. The man looked identical to Oliver. He had Oliver's face, his hair, and was even wearing his exact same outfit.

They stared awkwardly at each other for a moment. The little man seemed as surprised to see Oliver as Oliver was surprised to see the little man. Oliver wasn't sure whether he should introduce himself to the miniature version of himself or ask him politely who he was and what the hell he was doing inside his eye.

The miniature man waved at Oliver.

Oliver found himself waving slowly back at the miniature man.

There was another uncomfortable pause. Then the little man closed Oliver's eyeball door.

While sitting at his glossy white dining room table, eating a bowl of crunch berries with a grapefruit spoon, Oliver Madu heard hammering noises coming from his head. This was especially peculiar to Oliver, as he had never heard hammering noises coming from his head before.

Oliver tried to ignore the sounds, so that he could get through his morning routine uninterrupted, but the hammering made it nearly impossible for him to focus on reading his neatly folded newspaper and drinking his cup of French Vanilla Café.

At work, the noises only grew louder. There weren't just hammering noises, but drilling and sawing sounds coming from his skull as well. Oliver did his best to block these sounds from his mind, but they still got in the way of his concentration. The only thing he could fully focus his attention on was sitting upright in his chair with a professional posture while eating his powdered strawberry jelly donut with a fork and a knife. He didn't notice all the angry eyes glaring into his cubicle at him.

After a couple of hours, Oliver's boss called him into his office. He was a tall man with wavy blond hair, a dark orange tan, and big bright teeth. His hands were folded on a kayaking-themed mousepad calendar.

Oliver sat in a stubby chair on the other side of the desk, blinded by the iridescent lights reflecting off of his boss's teeth. The sound of drilling echoed through the back of Oliver's head.

"So, Oliver," his boss said with a half-smile. Oliver's boss always had a half-smile when he spoke. "I see your head is pretty noisy today."

Oliver nodded his noisy head.

"Care to explain why?" said his boss.

Hammers banged against the side of Oliver's skull.

"There seems to be some kind of construction going on in my brain," Oliver said, raising his voice so that he could be heard over the hammering.

His boss stood up and took a closer look at Oliver's head. He could see Oliver's hair shaking as the hammers struck.

"I see," said his boss, nodding. "Is there by chance any way you might be able to make it stop?"

Oliver thought about it for a minute. He looked up at the ceiling and stroked his thin beard. Then he shrugged.

"I don't think so," Oliver said.

His boss sat down and sighed.

"Hmmm..." said his boss, leaning far back in his chair with his fingers curled into his bangs. "You see, the thing is, these noises have been awfully disruptive."

Oliver nodded in agreement.

"There have been a number of complaints," said his boss.

Oliver apologized and wiped a patch of powdered sugar from his tie.

"Are you sure there isn't anything you can do to quiet down the noise?" asked his boss.

Oliver shrugged.

"I think you should take the rest of the afternoon off," said his boss. "Go see a doctor. Get this thing straightened out."

Oliver nodded his head as tiny hammers pounded against the inside of his temples.

By the time Oliver Madu got to the doctor's office, the sounds of construction had spread throughout his entire body.

"I don't know how to tell you this, Mr. Madu," said the doctor, examining Oliver with buggy eyes, "but it seems that you are not technically a human being."

Oliver loosened his nostrils. "What exactly do you mean by that?"

The doctor knocked on Oliver's chest. It sounded like he was knocking on a door.

"I'll probably need to do a few more tests to be certain," said the doctor, "but you appear to be made of wood."

"Wood?" Oliver asked, looking down at his chest.

"Oak, to be precise," said the doctor. "I've also been curious about these..."

The doctor lifted Oliver's shirt to reveal two little windows where nipples should have been.

"How long have you had these windows?" asked the doctor.

Oliver didn't recall ever having window nipples.

The doctor said, "The inside of your body appears to be hollow and home to fourteen miniature clones of yourself. These clones operate your body via a network of wheels and pulleys."

Oliver looked through one of his nipple windows to see miniature versions of himself walking by, wearing tool belts and carrying planks of wood.

"I'm rather certain that I am a human being," Oliver said, "I remember being human ever since I was a small child."

"Mr. Madu, I have been an authority on human anatomy for nearly twenty years. I think I know what I'm talking about in this matter."

"But I must protest," Oliver said. "I am not a robot."

"No, of course you're not robotic," said the doctor. "Actually, in comparison, a robot would be a far more sophisticated piece of machinery. You are a *simple* machine. You are more like a man-shaped ship than a human or a robot."

Oliver Madu was really bummed by the fact that he wasn't a human being. He decided the best course of action would be to get completely drunk.

At the local pub, he sat at the bar staring into a pint of honey ale. The construction noises had ceased for the day, but it didn't seem like that much of a consolation to Oliver.

As he drank his beer, the miniature clones in his chest busily collected it into wooden barrels. The mini-Olivers dunked their mugs into the barrels, filling them with honey ale. They guzzled the beer as quickly as possible, so that they could dip their mugs once more. By the time the fourth pint was empty, the Oliver clones were completely drunk and ready to party.

Oliver didn't know why his left arm kept jerking, knocking over his empty pint glasses. Inside his body, the little man responsible for controlling this arm was leaning back in a chair with his feet propped up on the control board. The little man was chugging a mug of beer and flipping through the pages of a nudie magazine called Chubbies. He didn't realize that his feet weren't doing a very good job keeping the wooden steering wheels steady.

Oliver's left arm raised straight up into the air and then went limp. He unbuttoned the top of his shirt with his right arm and looked down through a window nipple. Inside, he could see all the mini-Olivers drinking and partying. One of them had a little accordion and was playing hoedown music, as the others clapped and danced and raised their beers into the air.

A wooden groan poured out of Oliver's mouth as he re-buttoned his shirt. Then his right leg kicked over the stool next to him and spasmed in the air, as a mini-Oliver did a beer bong over his leg controls.

The other bar patrons wondered what the hell was wrong

with Oliver. College girls giggled at him. Old men glared at him with clammy eyes. After his leg stopped twitching, the fingers on his left hand started curling in and out of his fists of their own accord. He gulped down the rest of his pint, attempting to drown the little bastards. They danced with open mouths as the beer rained down on their heads.

Then both of Oliver's eyeballs opened up and he went blind. He felt two miniature clones of himself hanging out of his eye sockets, hooting and hollering, shouting, "Yeah baby!"

Oliver slammed his eyeballs closed, pushing the tiny drunks backwards. He felt them tumble down his throat. Then he saw what they were hollering at. In the eye of a woman across the bar, there was a drunken miniature version of that woman flashing her breasts at the bar patrons.

The woman at the bar slammed her eyeball closed and grumbled to herself. Then her eyes met with Oliver.

Oliver Madu found himself staggering towards the woman on the other side of the bar. The mini-Olivers were frantically working the controls, chugging beer, yelping excitedly.

"Come on, boys!" shouted the captain of the Oliver ship, cranking a wheel in the brain-shaped cockpit. "Let's go get some!"

The drunken clones were not in the right state to drive Oliver. They couldn't control his legs very well. They couldn't keep adequate balance.

Oliver found himself leaning half of his body against the edge of the bar as he was driven towards the woman. His head was rolling against his shoulder. He could hear his clones laughing and cheering as they stumbled over their controls. The other people in the bar gawked at him as he knocked over stools and ashtrays.

The woman had short black hair with a purple headband, purple lipstick, purple nail polish, and a purple dress. She was drinking a cosmo and trying to shush the clones giggling in her chest.

"Hi," Oliver said to her.

The woman smiled at Oliver. The sound of hopping drunken girls singing along to pop music boomed out from her cleavage.

He crashed down onto the stool next to her, and then tried to compose himself. He smoothed out the wrinkles in his beige suit with his sweaty palm.

"I hope you don't mind if I join you," he said.

The woman held out her hand. "Clara."

"Oliver," he said, grabbing her hand.

They didn't shake hands. They squeezed their palms together in a warm embrace.

The woman opened her mouth to take a sip of her cocktail. Before she could take a sip, a naked miniature version of her hopped out of her mouth into the drink. The tiny skinny-dipping woman squealed at the icy temperature as she swam through the pink fluid. She looked up at Oliver and waved at him.

Clara blushed as Oliver saw the naked version of herself. She quickly gulped down the drink and swallowed her clone back inside of her body.

"Excuse me," she said, and then giggled. She pressed her fingers against her cold wooden throat.

Oliver nodded.

The woman smiled at him, but her eyes darted down to her empty glass before he could smile back. Oliver looked at her purple fingernails wrapped around the stem of the glass.

He tried to change the subject. "So you like purple?"

Clara held out her hand to examine her fingernails.

"Oh!" Clara said, giggling, then she thought about it and frowned. "Uh... Not really."

"Oh," Oliver said.

A mini-Oliver climbed out of a window nipple and crawled out of Oliver's shirt. Then he fired a grappling hook at Clara, catching the collar of her dress, connecting them together by a thin black thread.

"So what do you do?" she asked.

Clara pretended not to notice the mini-Oliver as he climbed the thread towards her.

"I work in accounting," Oliver said.

"Really?" Clara said. "You must be good with numbers."

The mini-Oliver was halfway across the thread by the time Oliver noticed him. The tiny clone hooted at two mini-Claras who whistled at him from Clara's cleavage. The mini-Claras shouted, "Come party with us!" And the mini-Oliver yelled, "Yeah baby!"

"Not really," Oliver said.

He snatched the mini version of himself from the thread. The miniature man kicked and cried as Oliver shoved him down his shirt and through his nipple window.

"I work in human resources," Clara said, edging her knees closer to Oliver, as if the black thread was reeling her in.

"Nice," Oliver said, smiling and nodding.

The bartender came by and placed a turkey sandwich in front of Clara. He was a young man with pierced lips and a big round belly.

"Here you go," said the bartender. "Need anything else?"

"Oh," Clara said to the bartender. "Can I get a fork and knife?"

After the bartender acknowledged her request, Clara looked at Oliver.

"I eat everything with a fork," she said to him. "I don't like to touch food with my hands. Not even sandwiches."

Oliver's eyes lit up. "Me too!"

They stared at each other for a moment. They blinked slowly at each other and their lips curled into smiles.

Clara called out to the bartender, "Never mind. I think I'd like this to go."

Back at Oliver's place, Oliver and Clara sat together on his couch, half-empty wine glasses on the coffee table next to them. Their clothes were pulled up to their necks, their bellies opened up like barn doors.

All of their clones partied together on the couch, on their laps, on their shoulders. The mini-Claras danced drunkenly with the mini-Olivers. Some of them were making out. One Oliver clone held the hair of a Clara clone as she puked out of Oliver's nostril. One couple was already naked together in a closet in Clara's upper thigh.

Oliver and Clara lay motionless on the couch, gazing into each other's eyes. Their mouths were stretched into dazed smiles. Their wooden hands were folded tightly together between their hips. But because their operators were outside of their bodies, they were no longer able to move, talk, hear, see, feel, or think.

RED WORLD

The world's going through some changes. Something having to do with the sun oozing out a long trail of syrupy red snot that's been affecting our atmosphere. One of the major changes Earth has gone through is that it isn't as colorful as it once was. From space, it's no longer blue and green. It is red. A deep crimson that looks gory and obscene. Like a human heart pulsing slowly in space.

The colors that we see have also changed. As I walk down the street with my little brother, we can't actually see any blues or greens or yellows. The trees, the cars, the clothes of people passing us on the sidewalk, they are all shades of red. There are some purples and some oranges, but not in abundance. Looking at our mirror images in pizza shop windows, our skin is pomegranate-colored, our clothes are pink, maroon, and sienna camouflage, our hair like burgundy mops.

Nobody else realizes that we are covered in blood.

"Can we get some cinnamon ice cream?" Scooty asks, sticking his hands in and out of a mail slot.

I busy my eyes down the street, making sure nobody's following us.

"We don't have money for ice cream," I say.

Scooty pouts his cracked lips and kisses the tips of his fingers. He does this whenever he's nervous. I light up two cigarettes and pass him one. He breathes it in deep and points his mouth up at the sky before he exhales so that he won't get any smoke on his dress. He's used to getting beaten if customers smell smoke on his dress.

"Come on," I say, taking him around a corner. "I know a place we can hide out."

Scooty was always a weird little kid. We were never really that close. I only lived with him for the first five years of his life before I couldn't take Mom anymore and left home to live on the streets with my girlfriend. It's been four years since I last saw him. I just remember a scrawny little boy who always seemed to have rubber bands in his pockets and cheese whiz on his face.

His hobbies included: dipping his fingers in hot wax, sniffing at the vacuum cleaner, and making little doll people out of cigarette butts.

That's what I remember most about him: the cigarette butt people. He used to steal cigarettes out of Mom's ashtray and with a toothpick he'd poke eyes and a smiling mouth in the tan outer paper. Then he'd pull the paper down to reveal a smidgen of the tar-stained cotton filter that he would fluff out until it appeared to be hair. For arms and legs, he would break the toothpick into quarters and stick them into the sides of the butt.

Scooty didn't have any toys or friends as I did, so he had to make do with what his imagination could provide. His imagination provided dozens and dozens of ashy cigarette people living in castles made from stacked together beer cans.

Instead of saving it, Scooty tosses his cherry lipstick-glazed cigarette butt into the rain gutter after he finishes, so I'm guessing he doesn't make them into little dolls anymore.

"Want some turtle gum?" he asks.

He's staring up at me but I avoid eye contact, quickening my pace to get through a crosswalk.

His bloody fingers dip between his cleavage and he pulls out a falsie. The back of the silicon mound has been dug out so that he can hide things inside. He has a pack of gum, some stickers, rubber bands, a super bouncy ball, and a dead cricket stashed in the hole. After folding the gum into his mouth, he kisses the dead cricket and puts everything back into his bra.

I stop him, grab him by the shoulders. I take the falsies out of his bra and toss them into the street.

"You don't need these anymore," I tell him. "All that is behind you now."

"But my stuff..."

"You don't need any of it," I say, smearing the makeup across his face, trying to rub it off.

"Were you always so mean?" he asks, poking at me.

I take him by the wrist and continue on.

I used to be mean. Very mean, when I was a kid. But you're expected to be mean when you're as big as I am. I was kind of a freak growing up. Nearly twice the weight and height of everyone my age. The other kids were either scared of me or too eager to buddy up to me so that I could do them favors. By *favors* I mean they wanted me to hurt someone for them, either for revenge or for their entertainment. They saw me as some kind of bully for hire. All I asked for as payment was a bit of friendship, but I always seemed to get stiffed after the deed was done.

Beating other kids was not something I had a passion for. I admit that it was enjoyable, but what I enjoyed about it most was how happy it made the other kids who watched me pound my victims into the dirt. I was able to make them smile and laugh. That made me feel good. I would do anything to make people smile and laugh. It's too bad that all people ever wanted me to do was hurt other people.

So bullying wasn't a real hobby of mine. My real hobbies included: playing zydeco accordion, watching Japanese animation without subtitles, and hanging out during geezerball games.

Geezerball happened every Tuesday afternoon in West

Park. A bunch of old guys would get together on the court to play some of the most intense basketball games I've ever seen. What these guys lacked in talent and physical ability they made up for with an unrelenting passion for the game. They played with everything they had, with every ounce of strength, with every heartbeat of energy. They played as if they only had one afternoon left to live and each basket scored would make up for things they didn't accomplish in their lives; every missed opportunity, every lost love, every abandoned dream.

After school, we used to gather in the park to hang out and watch geezerball. The other kids loved to make fun of them. They laughed at the old men and threw balls of paper and soda cans when they missed their baskets. They hoped they would get a chance to see one of them have a stroke and die in the middle of a game. I went there just because I liked to watch the old guys play. Nothing I've ever experienced is as powerful as watching a game of geezerball.

"My feet are grapey," Scooty says, but I don't know what he's talking about.

He takes off his stilettos and rubs his blistering heels.

"It's just another block," I tell him, tossing his shoes away. "Then you can walk on grass."

He steps carefully down the sidewalk until we get into the park. We creep through the grass, making sure nobody is watching us as we go over the hill. The screeching wail of the cluster makes Scooty rub his ears. He frowns at the shifting red-black blob that stretches into the distance.

"I no like it," he says.

Besides turning red, the world has gone through many other changes. One of them is the change in insect behavior. For the past few years, bugs of all types have been gathering in clusters. Every dragonfly, cockroach, earthworm, grasshopper, millipede, bumblebee, mosquito, tarantula; all of them have been bonding into giant swarms. A collective that feeds together, breeds together, thinks and acts as a single entity. Clusters can be as small as a puddle or as big as a small ocean. The one here is the biggest in the city. It fills at least three miles of ground. All the buildings on this side of town have been abandoned, flooded by billions and billions of squirmy black creatures.

"Dead end," Scooty says.

"No," I tell him, "We're going through it."

I dig through the nearby bushes and uncover about a dozen pairs of stilts, most of them homemade out of old ladders and belts. I take a bright red-orange pair and climb the nearby tree.

"Come on," I tell Scooty.

Scooty cleans some mud off of some blades of grass.

I lower my hand and pull Scooty up into the tree with me. He wraps around my torso like a backpack. Then I lace my boots onto the stilts and carefully stand us up. I walk us slowly through the park down towards the sea of insects.

"Creaky," Scooty says about the sound, chewing on the back of my hair.

Then we enter.

I left home when I was fifteen because my mom called my girlfriend a whore and then broke her lip with a rum bottle. I'm not sure how the argument started. I think Mom accused Crissy of stealing cocaine out of her DVD player or maybe she had offered Crissy a line and was offended by her lack of gratitude. Not sure. I just remember that Crissy hit her back, with a croquet mallet, and after my mom hit the floor we kicked her in the stomach until she cried for us to stop.

Scooty was watching from behind a beer can castle. I wanted to say goodbye to him, tell him to take care of himself, but the moment was lost after Crissy kicked down his castle with her combat boot. She was always breaking my little brother's homemade toys under her combat boots. The last image I had of little Scooty he was covering his eyes so that he couldn't see his beer can structure in ruins.

Then Crissy and I were on the streets. Most of the time we were squatting, but some of the time we stayed at her older brother's apartment/meth lab. Four years of drug addiction, robbery, fist fights, abortions, withdrawals, punk shows, stilt-walking, foreign films, razor poker tournaments, and twitchy street performances followed. Three years of that was spent in the red, but I was so fucked up at that time I had no idea whether the red was real or just something wrong with my brain.

Crissy and I were sort of an odd couple. She was short and thin, smart, white, and listened to punk. Her hobbies included: drunken skateboarding, ballet, and razor poker—which is kind of like Texas hold 'em for sadomasochists. Instead of betting money they would bet blood, freshly cut from the body.

We knew our relationship would never last. She said that someday she would do something to piss me off so much that I would hit her. She said she would never forgive me if I ever hit her. Just one strike and our relationship would be over. I came close to hitting her, several times, but I never did lay a hand on her. The problem was with her crusty ass-faced brother, Jack.

One morning, I caught Jack raping Crissy in the shower. That wiry motherfucker with the curly hair and thin goatee had her pinned to the rim of the bathtub, blasting rap-metal in the living room, holding her head under the water and fucking her from behind. He was so far gone that he probably didn't even know what he was doing or who he was doing it to.

That image burned into me: seeing Crissy with her tiny fists punching at her older brother, her wrinkled eyes closed so tight they were purple, his chalky hands grabbing at her body. Something triggered inside of me. Until that day, I didn't know my own strength. Nothing had ever pissed me off enough to use my full strength. I grabbed Jack by his scabby little throat and tossed him out of the room like a pile of dirty clothes. His body crushed a hole into the wall in the next room. I picked him high off the floor. The ceiling fan crashed into his neck, breaking against his voice box. Then I punched him in the face until his eyes swelled shut and his teeth pointed backwards at his tongue.

At first, Crissy was happy I saved her. Happy that the son of a bitch got what he deserved. But after a few days she stopped seeing Jack as her rapist and remembered him as her brother. She saw all the pain he was going through, how badly damaged I had made him, how many staples he needed put into his face. She felt sorry for him. And she no longer wanted to have anything to do with me.

I left without a word. I went back to my mom's place, but her apartment building had been condemned. Nobody lived there anymore. I didn't know where else to go, so I checked myself into rehab.

Walking on stilts through the insect ocean, the bottom of my feet are only inches away from the surface. Crissy and I used to stilt-walk through the cluster all the time. It had been a popular thing to do for the past couple of years. A lot of junkies and homeless guys live out in the abandoned buildings here. The people who originally lived in them had to leave most of their belongings behind when they were evacuated, so there's a lot of good stuff to steal as long as you can carry it out on stilts. There's also a lot of furniture, so it's really good shelter if you're used to sleeping on the streets. It's also a perfect place to hide out when you're on the run. Cops never venture out into the cluster.

Unfortunately, stilting through the cluster takes practice. It's dangerous to enter it without mastering the stilts. A lot of people fall down in the cluster and unless they are near the shore they rarely survive. The insects won't bother you while you're stilting through, but if your flesh comes in contact with the surface they'll attack. They'll enter through your mouth, fill your lungs and drown you, then devour you inside out.

I've never tried stilting through with so much weight on my back. Scooty's so light I figured it would be no problem, but he's putting me off balance. I take small careful steps. The ground pulses, squirms, and hisses at me.

"It smells like purple mayonnaise," Scooty says.

Far ahead, there are figures on stilts walking between buildings. They move casually, as if walking through insects was as normal as walking down the sidewalk. The figures talk to each other as they stroll, waving at other stilters passing them down the street. The closest buildings appear to be a bit crowded. We might have to find a more secluded one farther down.

I'd prefer nobody knew we were here. I'd especially prefer to keep away from the junkies. I've been sober for a while now and I want to stay that way. Especially now that I've got Scooty to look after.

In rehab, my roommate was this fat crazy black guy named Ed. His hobbies included: reading gay erotic vampire novels, cooking Cajun food, and destroying everything that got in his way.

He also had a passion for huffing spray paint. He liked to go into back alleys and huff paint fumes until his vision went sparkly and his adrenaline started pumping. Then he would take out all of his aggressions by killing stray cats. He would stomp on them, break their necks, grab them by the tail and beat them against the wall until their insides were splattered across the dumpsters. Ed was just that kind of guy. He liked to hurt things. If it wasn't cats it probably would have been people.

I didn't like Ed very much, but for some reason we became friends. He was either gay or bisexual, I'm not sure which, and he always tried to get me to help him rape some of the smaller guys in the place. I used to tell him, "We're in rehab, not prison. What's wrong with you?" And he would respond with his usual response, "Ah, just playing with you." Whenever he said that his voice would be deep and angry, as if he really wasn't just playing with me.

Ed and I left rehab together. I was hoping I wouldn't have to see him again, but he took a liking to me—probably because I was the first person he'd ever met that was bigger than him. We got jobs lifting boxes for UPS and moved into a low income housing apartment that was so tiny it made me wish I was back in rehab. Ed was an unbearable roommate who liked to break all of our Goodwill furniture and stab holes in the wall with a lime-cutting knife. But if it wasn't for him, I probably would never have seen Scooty again.

Stilting through the sea of insects, we find a less popular apartment building. I stilt us to an open window and lean inside so Scooty can enter by climbing over my head. Then I pull myself inside, close the window, and remove the stilts. We're in a sweaty hallway, the paint dripping off of the ceiling in large sheets, mud caked on the carpeting. There is a pile of stilts in the corner. This must be a common point of entry. Most of the time the bugs are too high for us to enter through first floor windows. Usually we have to climb up to the second story, which is pretty difficult when you have long wooden legs.

I take off my stilts and lead us down the hall.

"This way," I tell Scooty.

All the doors are smashed in. Some are in splinters, others just have broken locks. We go into the nearest one. I set the stilts behind a sticky leather couch. The place is in decent shape. There's enough pink sunlight coming in to brighten the place. The furniture isn't trashed. Nobody has taken a shit in the corner. That's always a good sign. Many of the apartments that aren't occupied by vagrants tend to be transformed into giant bathrooms. Some people have the decency to shovel their shit out a window, but others just crap right on the carpeting and move on.

There's a dead junkie in the kitchen. He's not smelling up the place yet, so it must have happened recently. A bald guy with a scraggly red beard, wearing a lady's fluffy pink robe. The needle still in his arm.

He was shooting slice, which is very popular here in the cluster. It is as strong and addictive as heroin only it is a hallucinogenic drug that causes very realistic lucid dreaming.

That's another change the world has gone through: dreams have disappeared. Something in the atmosphere has stopped our ability to dream at night. Maybe some chemical in the air has interfered with our sleeping cycle. Maybe we can't reach REM sleep anymore. Crissy always said that it's impossible, that we'd all lose our sanity without REM sleep, that we wouldn't be able to function physically or mentally anymore. Maybe that's why slice is so addictive. People can't function without it. Personally, I don't miss my dreams. I don't remember any of them being any good.

"Let's get out of here," I say.

I turn around. Scooty isn't there.

I find him in one of the bedrooms of the apartment. A kid's room. It is filled with toys scattered all over the floor. His mouth is wide open like it's Christmas morning. He was always excited for Christmas morning, even though all he ever got, if he got anything at all, was some gum and maybe a couple chocolate cars that he was allowed to play with for a few hours before Mom wanted to eat them.

I'm surprised he's excited about toys at all. He's nine years old. Kids should stop playing with toys once they turn six.

"You can't have any," I tell him as he digs through the army men and plastic robots.

His face turns from a smile to a frown. He doesn't argue.

"Come on," I say, taking him out of the apartment.

Ed is the one who found Scooty for me. Yesterday, he was out fucking tranny whores when he saw my little brother in drag welcoming a middle-aged Asian cop into his bedroom. I'm not sure how Ed knew it was my brother. All he knew about my brother was that his name was Scooter and that he kind of looked like a short scrawny version of me. I'm not sure how he figured that out unless he had a conversation with him. And I'm not sure how he had a conversation with him unless he was in his bedroom. I tried not to think about it. All I cared about was that I knew where Scooty was and that he needed my help.

We went out to get him this morning. Scooty was living in a building Ed called The Twinkie Factory. It's in the northeast industrial area and I think there actually was a Hostess factory across the street at one time. The building was an old hotel turned crack hotel turned crack whore hotel. When we arrived, the door was operated by a large bearded guy with black teeth. He greeted Ed as if he were a regular customer. Ed wiped powdered sugar off of his big round belly, pretending he didn't know the guy.

"We want to talk to Scooter," Ed told him. "It's his little brother."

The man licked his whiskers at us. "No boy named Scooter here." He paused to spit onto his fingers and smell it. Then he gave Ed his sales pitch. "We have a fine selection of ladies available. Tell me what your heart desires. If your heart desires them big, we have them big. If your heart desires them fresh, we have them fresh."

"Look." Ed got into his face. "I know his brother is here. I saw him yesterday. Just let us see him and don't fuck with me."

"Get the fuck out of here," Black Beard pulled a gun on Ed and dug it into his squishy belly.

Ed looked down at the gun with an annoyed face.

"What do you think you're doing with that?" Ed pushed hard on the gun. "Think a bullet is going to stop me, bitch?"

The gun went off. Black Beard's face was surprised, as if it went off by accident. His mouth was wide open, exposing gums as black and tarry as his teeth.

Ed was pissed. He wrapped his arms around the guy, crushed all the air out of his lungs, and then rammed him against the side of the building. The gun went off again.

I couldn't see any blood. It was blending in with the redness of our vision. None of it seemed real to me.

All Ed could manage to say was "Motherfucker..." as he grabbed Black Beard by the throat and choked him.

It took less than a minute for Ed to kill the sorry bastard just by crushing his neck with both hands. But Black Beard had managed to empty the rest of his rounds into Ed's chest as he was being choked. They fell together. Both dead before hitting the street. All I heard was a slight grunt from my roommate as he hit the ground.

I stood there alone for a few minutes. Not sure whether to continue on by myself or run away.

"What the fuck was that?" I said to Ed's corpse.

He sure as shit could have handled that better.

A shirtless bald guy burst through the door with a gun in his hand. He fired at me but it just clicked. I jumped at him and threw my fist into his jaw. He was fumbling with his pistol, trying to take the safety off. I grabbed him by the trigger arm flipped him onto the ground, and then stomped on his head. He went limp. I probably just knocked him out, but he didn't look like he was breathing anymore.

His pistol was empty. The dumbass forgot to load it. Armed or not, I had to go in and get my little brother. Before I stepped one foot through the door, I could already hear the chaos going on inside.

As we leave the dead junkie's apartment, the sound of screeching insects fills the hallway. The window is open and somebody is coming in from the cluster. He is bald and wears a dark trench coat with big black goggles.

"Hey," he says to us as he enters.

He doesn't bother removing his stilts as he approaches.

"You don't live here," he says, staring down at us. "What are you doing here?"

"We're moving in for a few days," I tell him.

"We'll see about that," he says.

I'm ready to throw him out into the cluster without his stilts if he refuses.

"You'll have to get approval from the other residents," he says. "We don't just let anybody come in here and take over the place. We take care of our own."

He walks by us and enters the stairwell, still walking on the stilts. "Follow me," he says.

We follow him up the stairwell, but have to move quickly in order to keep up with him. He flies up the stairs, skipping six steps at a time. I've never seen anyone so maneuverable on stilts before. It's more like he's pole-vaulting than stilting.

"So what do I call you?" he asks.

"Jake," I say. "And this is Curtis."

I don't want him to know our real names.

"Charlie," he says.

He takes off his goggles to reveal large bulbous fish-eyes that take up a large portion of his face. Scooty takes a step back when he sees them. I grind my teeth.

Mutations are another big change the world has gone through over the past few years. The chemicals in the atmosphere that made the world red have also caused some of the DNA in certain people to transform into that of marine life, creating a new race of mutant fish people. It's only a small percentage of the population. Crissy said it was probably some kind of allergic reaction to the red. It's not something that people like to talk about, but we do have a lot of fishy-fleshed people walking around these days.

There were plenty of fishy-fleshed people in The Twinkie Factory as I entered to reclaim my little brother. Many of the whores had lobster tails or flipper hands. Many of the customers were scaly with shark fins for hair. I hate to think of what my brother went through servicing those bug-eyed freaks.

I went room to room looking for my brother. Most of the customers and whores were running crazy through the halls, not sure where the gun shots were coming from, assuming it was a gang shootout or cops were raiding the place. Some of them could tell I had something to do with it and got out of my way.

In one room, there was an enormous aquarium. Two fishy whores were swimming in there. Their DNA was so distorted that I don't think they could actually breathe out of the water anymore. An oxygen tank was on the floor, probably used by customers so that they could have sex with the fish girls underwater.

A tranny whore jumped me from behind, wrapping squid tentacles around my neck and waist. I slammed her against the wall and elbowed her in her wide inky eye that popped like a blackened egg yolk.

Two more fishy transsexuals jumped me. One burly freak with the head of an anglerfish and one with crab legs and claw arms larger than my torso. Angler Face pushed me into a corner as Crab Legs snapped at me with her claws. The tentacled bitch with the drippy broken eye stood up and screamed, flapping her squiddy limbs at me.

I grabbed Crab Legs by the arm and snapped it against my knee. Crab Legs screamed as I pulled the broken arm-shell off of her, leaving a long tube of white meat where the claw used to be.

I swung the red spiky arm over my head, and smacked Angler Face in the ribs. Then I knocked Crab Legs' face through a plaster wall. The plaster must have been old and weak. It crumbled against the crustacean's body, filling the air with white dust.

Something hard and solid hit me from behind. Right in the kidney. Knocked me down. I looked up and saw Tentacles with an aluminum baseball bat. Then Angler Face opened her giant fishy mouth over me. Her head ballooned outward six times its normal size, and the next thing I knew half my body was swallowed up inside of her sludgy neck. Tentacles hit me in the ass with the bat a couple times. It didn't hurt much. I wasn't sure if Angler Face was trying to swallow me or just hold me in place, but I was beginning to suffocate in there. Her little tongue was squirming against the back of my arm.

I struggled to force myself free, but Angler's skin was like rubber. I punched but it did not hurt her. So I grabbed her little fishy tongue and ripped it off.

Angler Face roared and spit me out of her gullet. Before she was able to run away I stabbed her through the belly with the broken end of the crab claw. Then I ducked out of the way of the baseball bat as Tentacles swung it with all of her might. It made contact with Angler Face's brain and a loud crack filled the room. I flexed my armpit around the bat and slammed the claw into Tentacles' neck. She screeched as the claw squeezed around her throat. Then I reached inside of the crab leg and gripped the thin white tendon inside. I pulled on the tendon with one strong rip like I was working a chainsaw, forcing the claw to snap shut and decapitate the squiddy shemale in one stroke.

The head popped off with surprising ease, releasing a fountain of sparkly red.

Charlie leads us to the uppermost floor.

"We prefer to live as high above the cluster as possible," he says.

The top floor is bustling with activity. Fishy children race each other from room to room. An old woman is playing an acoustic guitar while her husband accompanies on harmonica. All of the doors are wide open. One apartment is filled with hairy men barbecuing giant millipedes. One apartment is filled with piles of junkies shooting slice. Another apartment is a nursery filled with clamshell babies. A lot of the people here are walking around on stilts. Either they're practicing their stilt abilities to make cluster-traveling easier or they've grown so accustomed to using stilts that they feel awkward using their real legs.

"Wait here," Charlie tells Scooty.

Then he looks my way. "Come with me."

I follow him down the hallway to one of the apartments on the end.

"What're we doing?" I ask him.

"You're going to be interviewed," he says. "We want to know more about you. We want to know why you've come here, why we should let you stay."

A kid with shark teeth jumps in front of me and shoots a cap gun in my face. I raise my arm to punch him, but stop myself from following through.

"What was that?" Charlie asks as I release my fist.

"Sorry," I say to him. "Just a reaction. I've been on edge all day today."

Seeing all the dead fish-faced trannies at The Twinkie Factory made my stomach quake. I considered ducking into one of the rooms so I could puke, but there wasn't any time. I heard movement through the ceiling above and had to get ready to keep fighting.

Two men in red-brown suits charged down the stairs. Sunglasses covering their fishy eyes, shark fins on their head instead of hair.

As the leader reached the bottom of the stairs, I cracked his kneecaps open against the aluminum bat. I took his gun away and shot him in the face, then shot his friend twice in the chest.

"Scooty!" I called out as I climbed over their bodies to get up the stairs.

The place was pretty much abandoned by then. I found Scooty all alone at the top of the stairs, dressed in drag, wondering what was going on.

"You remember me?" I asked.

"My bro," he said.

I hugged him.

"You're all sticky," he said.

"I'm going to get you out of here, okay?"

He nodded and took my hand.

The interview takes place in Charlie's living room. Five old men on stilts staring down at me with fishy frowns. I tell them the whole truth about the events that led up to our arrival here. I even tell them that Jake and Curtis aren't our real names. They feel for my story and allow us to stay. I think they also like the idea of having somebody my size on their side.

They give me one of the apartments on the end. It has been mostly gutted of furniture and food, but it has a nice couch in the middle of the living room. I lie down on it and relax my bruised muscles. Scooty is making friends with the fishy kids out in the hall. He is a few years older than them but that doesn't seem to make a difference to anyone. Nobody asks why he's wearing a dress.

It isn't such a bad place. It's cold and filthy and full of fish people, not to mention in the middle of an ocean of flesh-eating insects, but it's still an okay place. Until everything blows over, this will do. Scooty is safe here. Maybe this place will be a good distraction for him. Maybe he'll forget all about the events of today. Maybe he'll forget all about Mom.

Outside of The Twinkie Factory, a group of whores were gathered down the road, smoking cigarettes and watching us. I walked Scooty in the other direction and took him around a corner.

"How'd all this happen?" I asked him.

He smiled at me.

"Where's Mom? Why aren't you at home with her?"

He pointed in the direction of The Twinkie Factory.

"We live there now," he said. "Mom works upstairs."

The realization made my ears pop. "Are you saying she knows about this? She's the one who brought you here?"

He nodded.

My fists clenched.

"She's upstairs right now?" I asked him.

He nodded.

"Wait here," I said, as calmly as I could. "I'll be right back."

I hid him behind a dumpster and retrieved the gun from my jacket pocket. Then went back to The Twinkie Factory.

I wake up to the sound of Scooty screaming. I jump off of the couch and run into the hallway. One of the junkies on stilts is grabbing at him, pulling on his dress.

"Give it to me!" screams the junkie through a mane of long pink hair.

Why the fuck wasn't I watching him?

"Get away from him!" I yell, charging down the hall.

I tackle the junkie's stilts and send him crashing to the

floor. Then I crawl up his wooden legs and punch him in the stomach three times.

More stilted vagrants fill the hallway, attracted to the clamor.

"The kid's got slice!" Pink Hair screams as I punch him in the stomach again.

The junkies swarm around Scooty like long-legged spiders. They grab at him, trying to get to something he has concealed beneath his dress. One of them lifts my little brother off the ground and shakes him like a piggy bank.

"Motherfuckers!" I charge them and slam my weight against their stilts to knock them down or break their stilts in half.

I punch one of them as he tumbles down towards me, busting his jaw through the side of his face. I stomp another in the chest as he squirms to get back on his feet. One of them kicks me in the face with a wooden leg and knocks me back. Then they all swing their legs at me, trying to keep me back as I attempt to rip their faces off.

A freezing cold pain shoots through my belly and I hit the floor. I feel my lower back and pull out a greasy steak knife. Somebody stabbed me from behind. I turn around to see Charlie. He's no longer on stilts and seems ravenous for slice. He pushes his way through the forest of stilt-legs and gets to Scooty. My little brother cries as the man pries open his fingers and takes his treasure away from him.

Charlie's face goes blank as he sees the tiny robot in his hands.

"He doesn't have any slice," Charlie says. "It's just a toy."

Scooty grabs at Charlie to get the toy back, but the other junkies break the robot into pieces just to be sure there isn't any slice in there somewhere. They give the pieces back to Scooty. The expression on his face is as if somebody just ran over his dog.

As the junkies disperse from the hallway, Charlie staggers over to me. His mouth trembles. He acts as if he has just lost a million dollars.

"I'm sorry," he says to me, patting me on the shoulder as I

wheeze in pain.

I try to hold the blood into my body.

"Don't worry," I tell him. "I deserved it."

Upstairs at The Twinkie Factory, I found Mom strung out in one of the bedrooms with some kind of jellyfish girl. Both of them were in their own little worlds, their mouths wide open, their tongues white and swollen. I wanted to confront her. I wanted to tell her what a worthless bitch she was. I wanted to threaten to kill her but then tell her that it would be a better punishment to let her live, because her living hell of a life is already worse than death. But it didn't happen that way. I didn't have to tell her she was a worthless cunt, because she already knew it. She was lying there showing me just how worthless she could be.

So I shot her. Both her and the jellyfish girl. I shot them, tossed the gun on the bed, and left. There was no fear or anger running through my head as I exited the building. I felt nothing. Apathy. Emptiness.

My mother had always been one of the most worthless human beings on the face of the planet. She had been addicted to pretty much every substance available to her since she was a teenager. Besides sleeping, fucking, and getting wasted, her hobbies included: watching boxing on television (boxers always turned her on), playing croquet around the house, and making homemade firecrackers.

She wasn't a very loving mother. She wouldn't even let us hug her. She said she was allergic to us and that if our skin came into contact with hers she would get sick and have to go to the hospital. I remember when I was really young, I was always afraid I might accidentally brush against her and put her in the hospital. I was extra careful not to go anywhere near her. There was a period of about sixteen months when I never even stood in the same room with my mother, not even for a second, and the only way I communicated with her was through the wall.

As a kid, one of the main memories I had of my mom was her purple toilets. She was always eating beets. I think it was her favorite food. She ate beets every day for breakfast and lunch and sometimes on the side with dinner. She ate so many that the insides of all of the toilets she used were always dyed purple. The toilet water was often purple. And if she ever left a turd floating in the bowl it was also a dark woody purple.

Strangely, I remember that purple shit more than I remember my mom. Since I couldn't get too close to her, the only closeness I ever had was sharing the same toilet, watching her purple shit swimming with mine.

Despite all the things she did to me and all the things she didn't do, I still loved her for some reason. I couldn't say exactly why, but I did love her.

I think about my mom as I bleed to death in the hallway. My eyes hurt because they are too dry to tear. Charlie left me here, went back to his apartment to re-stuff a doll for his daughter. He said he would take me to the hospital, but I'm too big to carry through the cluster.

Scooty is sitting across from me, playing with the broken pieces of his toy robot. He is safe now. This place might not be perfect, but it is better than what he had been doing. It is the beginning of something new for him.

"Are you having fun?" I ask Scooty.

"Yeah," he says, but doesn't look at me.

"That's good," I tell him. "Keep having fun."

I watch him as he plays. I have no idea what goes on in that mind of his. He's always been in his own little world. I envy him for that. He's always having fun without a care. He doesn't bother to acknowledge all of the horrible things that are always happening in this world.

He doesn't even realize that the red floor he is playing on is soaked with my blood.

HAMMER
WIVES

It took all day to find the entrance to the mansion. I found the property easily enough. It was only twenty minutes outside of McMinnville, the small town in which I'd been raised. But finding the front door of the building was not a simple task in the slightest.

"You're not really going *there* are you?" a hippie cyclist said after I flagged him down for directions. He had been riding his mountain bike down the country road when I came across him. He was the only person I had seen all day. "The place is a vortex, man."

"A vortex?" I asked.

"It's got bad vibes, man," he said, guzzling a kombucha. "It's bad for your soul."

"It's important I go there," I told him, but the hippie just shook his head and rode off into the woods.

The estate was vast. It was once the largest vineyard in the region, but now there was no room for vines to grow on the property. All of the land was occupied by an immense crudely-constructed wooden structure that looked much like a child's tree fort the size of two international airports put side-by-side.

The layout of the building was utter chaos. Doors and windows were crooked or upside-down. Driveways led to nowhere in particular. Garage doors appeared thirty feet off the ground, making them impossible to use for the parking and storing of automobiles.

If it weren't for the mailbox jutting awkwardly out of a white rosebush at the edge of the estate, I never would have found the small path through the garden that led to the front door.

"This has to be it," I said to myself as I tapped the door-knocker.

I heard the knocking echo throughout the hollow interior. It sounded cavernous within. Based upon what the place looked like on the outside, I could hardly imagine what it would be like inside. It took twenty minutes of knocking before anyone answered the door.

"You must be Jacob," said the old man in the doorway.

There was only one word to describe him: mangled.

His nose was broken in five places, his head so misshapen that it could barely fit into his shaggy blond toupee, and his crooked legs were unable to support his weight without the assistance of two black wooden canes—the handles shaped like king and queen chess pieces. I could hardly believe that this gnarled figure was a blood relative of mine.

"I haven't seen you since you were a baby," he said. "It's good of you to come. You're all the family I have left."

A desperate, pathetic smile appeared on his face. It was the smile of a man who thought he had finally obtained that which he had been longing for: a family. But if this strange guy thought I had any intention of developing a relationship with him he was sorely mistaken. There was only one reason I had come that day.

"I didn't even know my father had a brother until I received your letter last week," I told him.

He closed his eyes and nodded.

"Your father and I weren't very close," said the old man. "I had already left home by the time he was born. He was more like a nephew to me than a brother. It's a shame he died so young."

"I don't even remember what he looked like," I told him.

The old man just nodded again.

Then he stepped aside.

"Please, come in," he said, gesturing for me to enter his estate. Within seconds of stepping inside, I became overwhelmed by a sense of loneliness and dread.

The week before, I received a mysterious letter from a man claiming to be my uncle. His surname was Vinson, like my father's. His first name was Edward, the same as my grandfather.

"I thought you didn't have any uncles," Jessica said, lying on the couch in my boxers and unbuttoned work shirt.

"I don't," I said. "At least I don't think I do."

"What's it say?"

I ignored her and read it to myself, pacing through the kitchen of my apartment. In his letter, Edward Vinson stated that I was his only living relative and that he wanted to make me the sole beneficiary to his fortune.

"Holy shit…" I said.

"What?" said Jessica, using one of my couch cushions to scratch her upper back.

"He's putting me in his will," I told her.

Jessica sat up, suddenly attentive. "Oh yeah? Is he rich?"

"He doesn't exactly say, but knowing my biological father's family it could be more than I'd ever hope to make in my lifetime."

"Really?" She smiled wickedly. "And it's all ours?"

I laughed. "It's all *mine*, you mean."

She stood up and wrapped her arms around my waist, enveloping me in my own shirt. "Everything that's yours will become mine someday, once I break you."

"You haven't broken me yet," I told her.

"Oh, I'll break you," she said, and bit into my bottom lip.

Then she snatched the letter from my hand, knocking something out of the envelope.

"What's this?" she asked, picking it up from the floor.

"A plane ticket," I said. "He wants me to come visit him next week."

She held up the ticket and waved it in the air. "Just one? Where's mine?"

"It's just to Oregon," I told her. "You wouldn't have any fun."

"Are you kidding? I love Portland."

"He's in rural Oregon, not Portland. Rural Oregon is about as fun as Wyoming."

She stuck out her tongue and said, "Ewww."

I didn't want to tell her that it was actually in Willamette Valley, the middle of wine country. Jessica loved good wine and would have demanded I take her along. But she was between jobs at the moment, which meant I would have had to buy the ticket and pay for everything. I was already paying for her rent and didn't have much cash to spare.

"It'll just be a couple days," I said.

She held me by the back of my neck, "Don't you meet any rural Oregon girls while you're out there."

"Trust me," I said. "You have nothing to worry about."

"And try to invite your rich uncle to the wedding," she said. "Maybe he'll help pay for it."

"And what wedding is this?" I pulled back a little.

"The inevitable one," she said, pressing me closer to her.

"We'll talk about it after we've been together for a few more years."

She placed her forehead on my neck. "I don't think I can wait that long, even for you."

I weaved my fingers into her dirty blond hair and hoped she didn't see me smile. She had no idea that I had already purchased the ring. In a few months, on our anniversary, I planned to ask her the question. I'm sure she knew it was coming sooner or later, but I was trying my hardest to make it a surprise.

Everything inside my uncle's home was made of unpainted, unpolished wood: the floors, walls, and furniture. It was completely undecorated and smelled of sawdust.

"Why is it so dark in here?" I asked him once I realized the only light was entering from the doorway.

"We don't have electricity here," he said.

I laughed. "What are you Amish or something?"

There was a pause. During the silence, I looked around at all of the wooden furniture and wondered if he really could have been Amish.

But then he responded, "I just don't see the point of electricity anymore. Not in this place."

He handed me a lantern.

"Take this," he said. "I've grown used to wandering in the dark, but you'll probably need light to get around. It's a large place. It's easy to get lost."

"Tell me about it," I told him. "I sure got lost on the way here."

"Oh?" he said.

"I couldn't tell the front of the place from the back."

The old man thought about it and then nodded his head.

"No, I suppose you wouldn't have," he said. "It always changes."

The inside of the building was just as insane as the outside. Corridors went in all directions. Doors of all shapes and sizes were spread across the walls and ceiling. It did not seem to have been designed by an architect. It was as if designed by an army of deranged children who wanted to make a mansion sized fort. There were creaking noises all around, as the structure rocked in the wind. It sounded like an old ship at sea.

"Is this place safe?" I asked when I saw the walls visibly rocking from side to side.

The place looked like it could collapse on top of us at any minute.

44

"Sections do topple over from time to time," he said. "But I've never been injured in a collapse. It's usually the outskirts of the building that fall over."

"So it is dangerous?"

"We'll be safe where we're going. The dining area is at the heart of the building."

I nodded in agreement, but inside my head I was thinking the guy was a complete lunatic. My instincts were to turn around and walk right out of there, but I found myself pushing forward. I followed closely behind the crippled man as he dragged himself through the narrow passageways.

We went for what seemed like miles, navigating the hallways like rats in a maze. The deeper into the structure I traveled, the more I sensed the overwhelming loneliness. This was not the type of place one could live in happiness.

"How long have you lived here?" I asked.

"A long time," he said. "Ever since the day I was married."

I was surprised to hear the strange man had actually been married. Judging by his lonely nature, I assumed he lost her a long time ago.

"How long were you together?" I asked.

"I'm still married," he said. "It's been over forty years now. I was about your age when we were bound in matrimony."

"Really?" I was a bit stunned. "I assumed you lived alone in this house."

"No," he said, almost sadly. "I'm never alone. My wives are with me, always."

At first, I wasn't sure if I heard that correctly.

"My wives are eager to meet you," said the old man. "They've been looking forward to your arrival all week. I've hardly been able to settle them down."

I was quiet for a moment as he led me down the black hallway.

"Wives?" I finally asked, raising the lantern to his face. "You have more than one?"

The man smiled brightly.

"I have ten wives," he said. "They are all hammer wives."

"Hammer wives?"

He stopped and slowly looked back at me, a distressed look in his eyes.

"Are you saying you don't know about the hammer wives?" he asked.

He seemed upset by the confused look on my face.

"No," I said.

"But everyone in our family knows about the hammer wives," he said. "They're a part of who we are."

"Well, I have no idea what you're talking about," I said.

"So your father never told you…"

"I never really knew my father," I said.

The man turned away. He was fuming.

"Come with me," he said, scowling in the lantern light. "And whatever you do, remain calm around them. They're easily agitated."

The old man seemed clearly insane. If I thought I could have found my own way out of there I would have turned and ran at that very moment.

They were sitting at the dining room table, all ten of them, five on each side. Even within the dim candlelight, I understood why he called them hammer wives. These women, sitting so quietly and patiently around the table, had metal hammerheads growing from their necks.

At first I thought they were just hammer-shaped helmets, but quickly realized they didn't have human heads of any kind. There was nothing but hammer above the neck.

When they noticed we had entered the room, the ten

women turned to us. They said not a word. The black mouths on the front of their hammers could not move. They were only painted on to resemble lipstick.

"This is Jacob," the old man told them. "He's the nephew I've been telling you about."

The women didn't move from their seats, just faced me with their hammer heads. I didn't know what to say to them. They didn't seem like they could possibly be real living people. I wondered if they were some kind of human-sized marionettes, mechanical puppets being controlled by somebody beneath the table.

I found myself saying, "Pleased to meet you."

The women tipped their metal heads in a bow at me.

"Aren't they lovely?" said the old man.

My mouth was wide open.

"Come," he said. "Sit down."

My uncle pushed me with his canes toward a seat at the end of the table and sat me in the chair.

"Dinner will be served shortly," he said.

As I sat in the crooked wooden chair, the hammer women towered over me in the flickering candlelight. They were a good two feet taller than I was, not just because of the giant hammers growing from their necks but also because of their large-framed bodies that seemed to be built sturdy enough to carry their massive heads.

"Wine?" asked my uncle.

My mouth was still wide open. I didn't snap out of it until I saw him sit down at the other end of the table, facing me with his gnarled fingers folded together.

"Please," I said, ready to drink an entire bottle.

One of the hammer wives stood from the table and came to me with an unlabeled bottle of red wine. As she filled my glass, I diverted my eyes from her horrific metal head and realized what was below the neck: the woman had a perfect hourglass figure.

She was hardly clothed, wearing black lace underwear with matching gloves, scarf, and thigh-high stockings clipped to a garter belt. Her breasts spilled out of her corset, only inches from my face as she poured my wine. I found myself trembling in her presence, unable to take my eyes off of her. Warmth issued from her flesh, enveloping me, as if embracing me. I could see fluids pulsing through her pale arms. Moisture glistened against her bare shoulders and upper chest, below the black lace scarf.

That's when I realized these women were definitely real. They were not marionettes or machines. They were very much alive.

When my glass was full, I took a sip of wine. It was deep and oaky. Well-aged.

"Do you like it?" asked my uncle.

As he asked the question, my eyes were buried in his wife's cleavage. It took me a moment to realize he was talking about the wine.

"Oh, yes," I said, trying to regain my bearings. "It's very nice. Regional, right?"

When the woman moved away from me and sat with the others, I stared out across the table. All of them were dressed in the same alluring outfits. Although the lighting was dim, I couldn't take my eyes off of them.

"I have a large stock leftover from the vineyard that once thrived on this property," said the old man. "It's a fifty year old pinot."

"Really?" I asked, taking another sip. "It must be worth a fortune."

The old man took a gulp and groaned through his twisted lips. "In my opinion, it lost all of its complexity over twenty years ago."

I nodded my head, trying to pretend to be interested as my eyes crept toward his wives' half-exposed breasts. In my head, I knew they were grotesque monsters, but for some reason I found them incredibly arousing. It was beginning to frighten me. No woman had ever turned me on as much as they did at that moment.

I no longer wanted to run away. I wanted to stay there as long as possible. I wanted to learn more about these women with hammers for heads.

"You said you've been married for how long?" I asked my uncle.

"Over forty years," he said with a smile, as if pleased that I'd asked him about his wives.

"Then how old are they?" I asked. "They couldn't possibly be over thirty-five."

"They are forever young," said my uncle. "Haven't aged a day since we first met. But they're hammer wives. They never grow old. They never die."

I realized their hammers were turned to me, like they were watching me even though they hadn't the eyes to see.

"Forgive me for asking this," I said. "But what are they exactly?"

"What do you mean?" asked my uncle.

The women leaned in closer. If I had to guess I'd say they were insulted.

"They aren't exactly human…" I said.

A screeching noise echoed through the room as chair legs rubbed against the wooden floor. The women turned away from me, sitting up straight with their hammers pointed down at the table cloth.

"Don't be offended…" my uncle said to the women in a calming tone. "He's not as educated as I thought he would be."

The women jittered in their seats, scratching at the wooden table with long perfectly manicured fingernails.

"They're embarrassed by their distinctiveness," he told me. "They prefer their differences be ignored."

"I'm sorry," I said.

Their hammers turned to me, pointed at my head

"Don't be," he said. "I would have had to tell you anyway."
He took a sip of wine. Then he answered my question. "They
are pseudo-human."

"Pseudo-human?"

"They were engineered hundreds of years ago."

"So they are machines?"

"No," he said. "They are living beings."

"But they never grow old. How can they be living beings?"

"Yes," he said. "The closest thing I could compare them to
would be the mythological creatures known as vampires. Only
they are not evil, nor undead, nor were they ever human to
begin with."

"So how are they like vampires?"

"Vampires never grow old, but they will die unless they
drink blood."

"So your wives drink blood?"

"Not blood exactly."

"Then what?"

The old man smiled.

"Hold that thought." The old man stood from his chair and
two of his wives stood with him. "Our dinner must be ready."

"You're able to cook in this place without electricity?" I
asked.

"I can roast and boil food in the central fireplace," said the
old man. "The two of us will be having stewed rabbit tonight.
It's my specialty."

I nodded my head as he left the room. The old man said
that the stew was for just the two of us, so that would indicate
the hammer wives would not be eating. This did not surprise
me. They didn't have any mouths. But what was it about the
blood that they drink to stay young?

While I was alone with the other eight women, all I could
think about was how they were described as vampires. Vampires
with hammers for heads? They stared at me with their blank
metal faces. I couldn't imagine what they were thinking about,

if they could even think at all.

I took another drink of wine, then stared back at them. The longer I looked at their heads, the more I realized that the hammers were part of the reason I found them sexually appealing. The warm metal was in some way seductive. It made them seem dark and dangerous. Deadly. A hammer was not just a tool but a weapon.

Then I became erect while imagining what it would feel like to be hit square in the chest by one of their hammerheads. The thought of them crushing my bones caused me to breathe rapidly, my heart pounding. When I realized what I was fantasizing about, I brushed the thought away and laughed to myself. It was not the kind of thing that would have ever turned me on. The wine was much stronger than I realized.

"Dinner is served," my uncle said upon his return.

One of the hammer wives served me the stew. As she poured the meat slop into the black bowl in front of me, she rubbed a breast against my cheek. At first, I thought it was an accident, but then she did it a second time, leaning in so far that she could firmly press my chin into her cleavage.

For a second, I was lost within the smooth texture. Her flesh seemed softer than that of normal women, more delicate. Then I realized what was happening and I pulled away.

I went for the spoon and took a large bite of meat. A tiny rabbit bone immediately stabbed me in the cheek.

"How is it?" my uncle asked.

I pulled the bone out of my mouth. All I could taste was blood.

"Good," I said.

"It's a little cold," he said. "The fire was low."

I just nodded as I held the side of my mouth.

Before the old man sat down to eat, he went back to the

kitchen with two of his wives. They returned carrying several small cages and placed them one at a time on top of the table. Although it was too dark to tell what exactly was in them, I could see the rustling of live creatures through the bars. I also heard hissing, squeaking noises.

"What's all this?" I said.

"Their dinner," said the old man. The women opened their cages and released the critters from captivity. They were not any earthly creatures I recognized. There were two-headed rodents with bird-like beaks, furry snakes with eagle claws for limbs, turtles with spiked shells, rabbits with tentacle legs. All of them were small animals that seemed a hybridity of mammal, reptile, bird, and fish. They did not appear of this world.

"What are they?" I asked, pushing myself away from the table.

"Livestock," said my uncle. "We raise them ourselves."

"Livestock? These creatures?"

"Hammer wives prefer to raise and kill their food themselves."

I fell backward out of my chair as a hammer slammed into the table. The noise exploded in my eardrums. When I got to my feet, I saw that a turtle had been crushed beneath one wife's hammerhead, its body cracked open like a walnut.

Another bang caused me to leap as a hammer came down onto a long-haired frog. The woman struck so fast I didn't even see her move.

"It is the way they eat," my uncle said.

Then all of the hammer wives were slamming their heads down at the table. They attacked repeatedly, so fast that it sounded like machine gun fire. The table cracked and splintered, the whole room rumbled like a minor earthquake. Blood sprayed like a mist through the candlelight.

I stepped away from the table with my mouth open. The mutant critters shrieked as they were bludgeoned to death. Some of them tried to run, but didn't get as far as the edge of the table. The wives were precise and deadly with their hammerheads.

"Sit down," said my uncle.

Looking across the table at him, he seemed angry by the way I was reacting. He was sitting calmly, eating his stew despite the juices splashing out of the bowl as the table rumbled.

I returned to my seat at the table when I saw a two-headed rodent squealing toward me. It was making its way to the edge, dodging through the mess of mashed animal carcasses.

The thing came right at me, as if to use my body as shelter from the hammering predators. But one inch from the edge of the table and the hammer woman to my left slammed her head down onto its small body. Blood and green fluids sprayed into my face as it popped beneath the wrecking ball of a head. If my hand had been on the table at the time, all of the bones in my fingers would have crumbled to dust.

When the hammering was finished, and all of the creatures were reduced to puddles of soupy meat, my uncle explained it to me.

"They don't have teeth," he said. "So they chew their food outside of their mouths."

I wasn't sure what he meant by that.

"They have mouths?" I asked.

But he didn't have to answer. I could see for myself.

The hammer wives removed the lace scarves from around their necks, revealing tiny faces on the centers of their throats. With spoons, they scooped up the meat soup and tucked it within the tiny toothless mouths on their necks. Slurping noises filled the room as they guzzled down the bloody goop.

"Of course they have mouths," said my uncle. "They cannot speak or chew with their mouths, but they can drink and breathe."

I couldn't take my eyes off of their tiny little faces. They reminded me of the faces on dolls—cartoonish and creepy.

"Please don't stare at their faces," said my uncle. "They are very embarrassed of them. It is why they always keep them covered. People tend to find them unnerving."

"I'm sorry," I said, though unnerving was exactly the word I would use to describe them.

After a moment of contemplation, I had to dig further.

"Why don't they just eat pre-mashed food?" I asked him. "Instead of smashing things to death, they could use a blender or something like that. It wouldn't be as violent and messy."

My uncle shook his head.

"Would you want to eat a cheeseburger after it was put in a blender?"

"No," I said.

"That's what it would be like for them," he said. "Crushing their food themselves is part of their eating process."

Two of the women stood up and left the table.

"Besides, they love hammering," he said. "They can't get enough of it." He pointed at the ceiling with his gnarled fingers. "You've seen the size of this great mansion. My wives built it all themselves. They're obsessed with hammering. They hammer all the time, day and night."

The two women returned with more cages of animals. They were about to have seconds.

As the creatures were released from their cages, my uncle said, "But they especially like to hammer living things. They find it sexual. Crushing soft flesh with their metal heads turns them on like you wouldn't believe."

"Turns them on?" Those words were horrifying to me.

"Like vampires, they don't need food in order to survive, but my wives still find the process of eating to be pleasurable. Very pleasurable."

Then he stopped speaking as the thundering sound of hammering filled the room. I watched as the tiny creatures were crushed by the hammers. At first, I was repelled by the sight. But then I understood what my uncle had been saying. As they hammered, the women seemed to be moaning in ecstasy. They were sweating, trembling as they slammed their upper bodies back and forth. It was like they were having sex. Their nipples were erect and gently rubbing against their corsets. Their fingernails gripped their thighs as if they were about to burst into orgasm.

And as I watched them crush the poor defenseless creatures, I found that I, too, was becoming aroused by the experience. I imagined myself as one of the critters lying helpless before the might of their enormous metal heads.

Something was wrong with me. I felt drugged. There could have been something slipped into my wine or food, but I definitely didn't feel like myself.

After the dinner was over and the women returned their scarves to their necks, covering their miniature faces, I decided it was time to cut to the chase so that I could get out of there as soon as possible.

"So you asked me here for a reason," I said to my uncle, trying to compose myself. "You said you wanted to put me in your will."

He nodded at me.

"Yes," he said. "I am an old man. It is time for me to pass my fortune to an heir. You are the only candidate for this gift."

"I apologize for my bluntness, but how much exactly are we talking about?" I asked. "After your departure, that is."

"No need to apologize," he said. "This is why I sent for you." With his sleeve, he wiped rodent guts from the tabletop in front of him. Then he pulled out a long piece of paper and placed it on the spot he cleared. "This land will become yours, this house, and everything in it. I have more money than I could ever use, which is also yours. You'll need the money to buy lumber. There is never enough lumber."

"Why do I need lumber?"

"The hammer wives are constantly adding to the house," he said. "They'll need supplies. Plenty of supplies."

"The hammer wives will stay?" I asked.

"Of course they will," he said. "They will not die with me. They live forever, as I mentioned."

Inside my head, I was snickering. I had no intention of keeping the property or buying lumber for these strange creatures. I just wanted the money he had in his bank account.

"Very well," I said to him.

He pulled out a pen and pointed it at the paper in front of him.

"Then sign here," my uncle said.

I went toward him—trying to keep my eyes off of the towering half-naked women I passed along the table—and took the pen from his twisted fingers. He pointed at the bottom of the paper. Although covered in shadows, I saw the line he was pointing at, and signed my name.

"Let me give you some more light," said the old man, bringing a candle toward the contract.

The paper illuminated the second I finished signing. That's when I realized it was not an ordinary contract. It was an ancient parchment written in a language I didn't understand. There were arcane symbols drawn in what looked like blood. It must have been created generations ago, before America was even a country.

I pulled away from the paper and realized my fingers were bleeding. The pen in my hands was lined with small hook-shaped razors along the edge. They had cut into my skin and drawn my blood into it to be used as ink. I had just signed the contract in blood.

"The transfer is complete," said the old man with a smile.

The hammer women chirped at each other in their seats, scratching against the wood of the table with their fingernails.

"Wait a minute, what was that I just signed? I thought it was your will."

He shook his head. "My lawyers have already taken care of that. I turned over all of my assets to your name as of last week.

What you just signed was the marriage contract."

"Marriage contract?" My voice echoed through the room.

"Congratulations," he said, pulling himself to his feet to shake my hand. "May your ten beautiful brides provide you with great joy for the rest of your life."

"No…" I backed away. "You didn't say anything about marrying your wives."

"Of course you would marry them," he said. "That was the whole point."

"What do you mean it was the whole point? You never said anything about this."

"The hammer wives have been passed down through our family for generations. My grandfather passed them down to me and now I've passed them to you."

The women turned their hammer heads to me.

"No, thank you," I said. "I already have a woman I love. I was going to propose to her soon."

"But you're not married yet, are you?"

"Not yet."

"Then it's too late for that," said my uncle. "You already signed the marriage agreement. You are to be their husband for the rest of your life, bound by your blood, sealed by our gods." He pointed to an altar in the shadowy corners. It was a statue of tentacled beasts curled together around a human man and ten hammer-headed women. "At midnight tonight, I will pass on from this life and you will take my place as the head of this manor. There is no way out of this."

The hammer women stood from their seats. I tried to keep my distance.

"I'm sorry, but I'm in love with somebody else," I said.

"You are allowed to have mistresses," said the uncle. "You are encouraged to mate with other women so that they can marry your offspring after your death. But you cannot marry another woman. You will always belong to the hammer wives."

I shook my head.

"You'll have to find somebody else," I said. My eyes were tearing. "You must undo the contract and find somebody else to marry them."

"There is nobody else," said my uncle. "You are the last of our bloodline. You're their only hope."

The hammer women crept behind me faster than I saw them coming. They surrounded us.

"Fuck our bloodline," I said. "Find somebody else."

"They will die without you," he said. "I told you they are like vampires who require blood to live. But it's not blood they drink. It is something they can only get from men of our bloodline."

The uncle began to remove his shirt.

"Let me show you," he said.

His naked body was covered in dents and scars. His muscles twisted under his skin. I didn't realize it until that moment, but all of his disfigurements had been made by only one thing— the impact of giant hammers crushing his flesh.

"They did all that to you?" I said, pointing at his naked skin.

"They like to cover me in their kisses," said the old man.

Three wives slammed their heads into his back and chest. He smiled with satisfaction as his bones cracked beneath his skin, but he remained on his feet.

"Let me feed you one last time," the old man said to the women.

The three who had hammered him pressed themselves against his body, rubbing his flesh with their human hands. They pulled down their corsets to expose their breasts.

"This is how you must feed them," he told me.

As they rubbed his flesh, several tongue-like ropes of meat emerged from his nipples and shoulder blades. The woman in front of him lowered her breasts toward him. Her nipples unfolded like flowers opening to the sunlight, revealing two gaping throat-like caverns that hissed and salivated in my direction.

Like mouths, they closed around the old man's chest tongues and suckled upon them. The crippled man moaned as if it were more pleasurable than any natural sexual experience he'd ever had. The women behind him opened their nipples and drank from the tongue-organs on his back.

"What the fuck are those things?"

The old man grabbed onto one that wasn't being suckled and squeezed it. A grayish fluid squirted out and drizzled down his white chest hairs.

"It is the liquid that keeps them forever young," he said. "Only members of our bloodline possess these organs. That is why you are the only one who can possibly take my place. You must feed the hammer wives."

"I don't have those organs," I said.

The old man closed his eyes and sighed as the towering women drank from him.

Then he said, "All males of our bloodline are born with these organs. They produce milk for our wives."

He licked his lips as he said the word *milk*.

"Well, I wasn't," I said, cringing at the scene before me. "I'll show you."

I unbuttoned my shirt and exposed my chest to him.

"See," I said. "Nothing. I'm not the same as you. I might not even be a member of your bloodline."

Then I felt large soft arms wrap around my chest as a hammer woman groped me from behind. She rubbed her fingers against my chest and nipples. Four of them closed in on me.

"Tell them to let me go," I cried. "I'm not like you. I don't have those freakish things on my body."

As I was squeezed and caressed by the massive women, I became erect. My penis hardened, digging into the side of my pants. But that wasn't the only thing that was becoming erect. I felt my nipples swell. The pressure built until the skin tore open and wet tongues burst out.

"What the fuck!"

The moist appendages snaked through the air, out of my control, like worms trying to find earth to burrow into. And before I could stop her, a hammer woman pulled down the top of her corset and slipped my slimy new organs into her breasts.

I shrieked. Not in agony but shock as I felt fluids being sucked from my body into hers.

"Yes," moaned my uncle. "Nourish your brides. Your milk is young and fresh. It must be so sweet and delicious to them."

The sensation of being sucked was like nothing I had felt before. It was disgusting yet sexual and strangely satisfying. Something deep inside of me was taking over, telling me this was the purpose of my life. It was the sole reason I was born into this world.

But then I looked up at the hammer woman as she fed on me. Her tiny eyes peered at me through her lace scarf. It was like the face of a creepy doll with a look of ecstasy in its eyes. This was not the life I wanted. I loved Jessica. I had a future—a *normal* future that didn't involve breast-feeding hammer women until I was a mangled old man.

"Get off of me," I yelled.

My leg practically dislocated itself at the knee when I kicked the large woman away. Her hammer head flailed as she stumbled backward. My grotesque alien organs slipped out of her breast mouths and wormed through the air, squirting gray fluids down my torso.

I thrashed until I broke free of the women grabbing at me. Then I pulled my shirt closed, the tongue-organs squirming under the fabric as I buttoned it up.

"I don't care if I signed a contract," I yelled. "I don't care if I'm the only one who can keep them alive. I refuse to be married to them."

The women slowly backed away. Even the ones feeding from my uncle removed their breasts from his appendages and stepped back. The wrinkled teat-like organs sprayed gray milk across the floor.

"I'm leaving," I said.

"You can't leave," my uncle said, softly. "Without you, they'll die…"

"I don't care," I said. "Let them die. It doesn't concern me."

All ten of the hammer wives bent their heads back and screamed. High-pitched wails issuing from their tiny mouth holes filled the room, piercing my eardrums. Then they disappeared, running off in all directions, vanishing into the shadowy corridors.

The old man had a terrified look in his eyes. His mouth was wide open as he looked around the room in a panic.

Then he put his shirt back on and said, "You've offended them."

Hammering sounds erupted all over the mansion—above us, below the floorboards, through the hallways. The hammering was so fast that it sounded like a warzone of thundering machine gun fire.

"What's going on?" I said, trying to figure out exactly where the sounds were coming from.

"They're very upset," he said. "They always hammer when they are upset."

He staggered on his canes toward me.

"You should leave and come back later," he said, "after they calm down."

"I'm going to leave," I said. "But I'm never coming back."

"Follow me," he said.

Then he led me into the hallway, to take me back the way we came in.

Hammering sounds were all around us as we moved as quickly as we could through the hallway. The walls shook. The shadows flickered in the lantern light.

"This isn't good," said the old man. He was visibly sweating as he staggered down the hallway, his eyes twitching. "This isn't good at all."

"What are they doing?" I asked, following closely.

"Hammering," he said. "Hammering like crazy. I've never seen them like this before. There's no telling what they might do."

When we arrived at the front door, he stopped and turned to me, blocking my path.

"Were you serious when you said you would break your marriage contract and leave them?" he asked me. "If I let you walk through this door, do you really intend to let them die?"

I stepped away, keeping my distance. He had such a serious look in his eyes. I was afraid of what would happen if I answered incorrectly.

"Yes," I told him, unable to lie. "I don't care what happens. I will not be their husband."

"Then take me with you," he said with a desperate look in his eyes.

That was not what I was expecting to hear him say.

"Take you with me?"

"At midnight, my marriage to them will be annulled," he said. "Then they will come for me. They do not allow their ex-husbands to live on once they remarry."

"They'll kill you?"

He grabbed my shoulder with his gnarled fingers.

"But now I can be free of them," he said. "I can live the final years of my life however I want."

The hammering sounds were now so loud that I could barely hear him.

"I thought you cared about them," I said.

"I do," he said. "But they don't want me anymore. They want you. I have nothing left—"

His voice was drowned out by the thundering hammer sounds. Then there was silence.

"What happened?" I asked.

His eyes were wide.

"They stopped hammering," he said.

He seemed afraid to turn the doorknob.

"Let's go," I said. "My car isn't too far."

When my uncle opened the front door, there was no longer a garden out there. It was another hallway.

We stepped through the door into the new passage.

"What is this?" I asked, holding up the lantern to see as far down as I could. The hallway seemed to go on forever.

He leaned against a wall. A look of dread on his face.

"It's begun," he said.

I felt the wood. It was fresh, still covered in sawdust.

"Where are we?" I asked. "Did we get lost?"

He shook his head.

"This is a new addition to the house," he told me.

"Are you saying this really is the front door?" I said, grabbing the doorknob.

"They just built this area."

"That quickly?"

He nodded.

"They're trying to prevent you from leaving," he said.

"They built a new wing of this house so that I couldn't leave?"

"They'll die without you," he said. "They can't afford to let you escape."

Then he moved forward, continuing into the newly built section of his mansion.

"But how could anyone build this so quickly?"

"Hammer wives are not natural beings," said my uncle as he moved. "Each one is like a living tornado of construction. They can sweep across the land, leaving structures and houses in their wake. If they had the supplies they could rebuild an exact replica of Manhattan in less than a week. Constructing a new wing of this house would take them only minutes."

"How is that possible?" I asked.

"As I said, they are not natural beings."

Then we continued on, moving through the new hallways that even my uncle could lose his way within.

For hours, we wandered in circles while the sound of hammering echoed in the distance. The hallways went in all directions. There were dead ends and staircases that lead to nowhere. It was a maze that was constantly being built around us.

"Any idea where we might be?" I asked.

He leaned against a wall to catch his breath and shook his head. He looked like he was ready to give up already.

"They've probably rebuilt the entire mansion by now," said my uncle. "Even if I knew what part of the property we were on, I'd not be able to direct us. The layout has been completely redesigned."

"We have to keep trying," I said.

"It's no use. They can build faster than we can walk. We'll never get to the end. They'll just rebuild and rebuild. We'll walk in circles forever."

"I'm not giving up," I said.

"It's almost past midnight," he said. "Once that happens, they will come for us. They will kill their old husband and break in their new one."

"Break in?"

He smiled crookedly and held up his twisted arm.

"I told you they like to hammer things," he said. "On your wedding night, they will literally break you in. You'll never walk the same way again."

"Then we don't have time to sit around," I said. "We need to keep going."

I continued on, not waiting for the old man to get to his feet.

As we continued walking, the passageway became narrower and narrower.

"You know they're leading us this way, don't you?" said the old man.

"I don't know where else to go, do you?"

"They are building our path in front of us," he said. "So they can control exactly where we go."

"Then let's go through the walls," I said.

The old man laughed as I pushed against the wood.

"You won't be able to break through any wall built by the hammer wives with just your bare hands," he said. "Only the backs of their heads can pry these boards open."

I held up my lantern. Part of me was tempted to go back the way we came, but there was hammering in that direction. I knew they were building walls back there, closing off the path behind us. There was only one direction to go. Even though it was exactly where they wanted us, it was still the only direction available.

"Let's just keep going then," I said.

The path seemed to be curling into a spiral. It was at a constant inward curve. We weren't getting closer to an exit. We were getting closer to the middle, right into the heart of the wooden fortress.

The further we walked the narrower the walls became, and the lower the ceiling sloped downward, the higher the floor sloped upward. We could no longer walk side by side. We had to walk in a line. I didn't want to get trapped behind the old man, so I led the way.

"It's getting tight," I told him.

I found myself needing to walk sideways through the passage, crouching so my head wouldn't brush against the ceiling.

"They're not only restricting where we go," he said. "They're also trying to restrict our movement. We won't be able to run in these tight spaces."

We kept moving. The further in we went, the more dim the lantern light became.

"It's getting dark," I said.

"There's not enough oxygen to feed the flame," said the old man.

He was right. I was finding it difficult to breathe.

"We're running out of air?"

"These walls are airtight," he said, tapping them with one of his canes. "By now, there have probably been hundreds of walls built around us in all directions, and dozens of stories built above. Essentially, we are buried alive."

"They can suffocate us?"

"I'm sure that's not their intention," he said. "They just want to build an impenetrable prison around you, several layers thick—one that you couldn't possibly hope to escape from."

"I'll find a way out," I said.

"You can run in their maze all you want," he said. "But eventually they will break you."

"Let's go back," I said, pushing him out of my way.

He laughed and turned around. We went back the way we came, but after a hundred feet we came to a wall.

"See," he said, chuckling. "Dead end."

I put my hand on the wood. It was just as solid as any of the other walls. We weren't getting through here.

"You might as well give up," he said, looking at his watch. "It's now past midnight. They've won. They'll be coming soon."

"Not yet," I said.

"Go ahead and keep going," he said. "This hall will just keep getting smaller and smaller, and they'll keep building walls behind you every step of the way. Eventually, you'll find yourself in the center of this maze in a tiny coffin-like box that they'll keep you in for the next ten years or so until you learn to love them like a proper husband."

I sighed as I returned to the direction they wanted me to go in.

66

My uncle said, "It's what they did to your great grandfather when he tried to leave them for his mistress."

I ignored him and pushed forward, trying to get to the end of the maze as soon as I could. The old man was falling behind, but I didn't care to let him slow me down anymore.

"It's a good thing for us that my father was already born at that time," he continued. "What the hammer wives did to his mistress, my grandmother, when they caught up to her was—"

His words were cut off by the deafening sound of hammers behind me. I turned to see a wall being instantly erected between us. Within seconds, they had opened up the side of the wall and reconstructed it to block his path.

I dropped to the ground to see what was going on, looking through the opening that had yet to be hammered into place.

"Goodbye my lovelies," the old man said to the hammer women.

The area was being reconstructed around him, making a large enough space for them to gather. They surrounded him, circling him like sharks, then they attacked. As if he were a small mutant rodent being served for dinner, the women bludgeoned him to death. They hammered his corpse until his flesh was pulverized, his bones were powder, and all that was left of him was a meaty soup on the floor.

Just before the last board was nailed into place, blocking my view of the scene, I saw the hammer wives remove their scarves and drink his mashed flesh through the tiny mouths on their necks. Within moments, his corpse would be gone without a trace.

I didn't leave right away, just lying on the wood floor, listening through the wall, haunted by the sounds of the strange women slurping my uncle's remains down their freakish throats.

Moving forward seemed pointless. The old man was right.

It would just get smaller and smaller until I was trapped inside a tiny space in the center of the wood prison. But I didn't want to give up.

I thought of Jessica. I couldn't bear the idea of never seeing her again. She always said that she would break me one day and I'd marry her. I wanted that. I wanted her to be the one to break me, not these monsters. There just had to be another way out.

The only thing that came to mind was to get out the way the hammer wives were getting in. They had to take down walls in order to build new ones. If I could somehow get out as they were getting in, I might be able to find a new path other than the one they wanted me on.

"Or maybe there's another solution…" I said to myself.

I leaned against the wall. They were still in there, sucking fluids from the floor.

"So I'm the last of my bloodline am I?" I said to them. "If I die so do all of you?"

There was silence through the wall. They had stopped what they were doing to listen carefully.

I threw the lantern as far as I could down the hallway. It shattered against the floor, exploding into a pool of fire.

"This place is all wood, isn't it?" I asked. "It must be insanely flammable. I wonder how long it will take to burn it all down…"

There was silence for a moment. The flames spread, catching the walls on fire. Smoke crawled across the ceiling toward me.

Then the women squealed in panic, the same noise they made when I refused to marry them. Hammering sounds erupted around me. The walls opened up as they removed boards lightning-fast with the backs of their heads.

As the shrieking women went for the fire, I crawled between them and ran in the opposite direction. There was a path behind them that they had been using to traverse the maze with ease. Although I no longer had a lantern to light my way, the blazing fire was enough. It raced through the wooden maze faster than the women could break down the boards and hammer out the flames.

As I ran, the hallway widened out. I was no longer in their maze. I was now in the tunnel designed for easy access across the estate. It was a direct path out of there. The women were too busy fighting a fire to rebuild a new maze in front of me.

Up ahead, the hallway was not complete. The floorboards had yet to be put in place.

"What's this?" I asked.

It was dark up here. The fire was too far back to see what was before me. I kneeled down. Where the floorboards would have been, I felt asphalt. It was a driveway. I was near the edge of the property.

"Almost..." I said.

I followed the driveway until I reached a large black object resting in the middle of the path. Squinting my eyes, I could almost make it out. It was the front of a motor vehicle.

"My car?"

I didn't recognize it at first, because it was only a rental, but it was definitely the car I drove in with. The hammer women had added on such a large addition to the mansion that they built around my vehicle. Since they never expected I would take their maintenance passageway, they left it intact.

The key was still in my pocket. I got inside and turned on the engine. It purred to life.

"You beautiful, beautiful Toyota Corolla," I told the car. "The most reliable machine on the planet."

The headlights illuminated the hallway, revealing two hammer women running toward me, screeching in a panic. I put the car in reverse and hit the gas.

The hammer women were fast. They caught up to me before I could turn the vehicle around. One of them ran right in front of the car and slammed her head into the hood, denting it in three places. The other slammed through the back windshield.

"Fucking bitches!" I cried, as the glass showered across the street.

I slammed on the gas, driving directly into the woman in front of the vehicle. She hammered on the hood twice more before she was thrown into the wall. The bumper crushed her legs below the knees and she crumbled to the ground.

Backing up and turning around, the other hammer wife smashed open the side window, tearing through the metal roof as if it were as fragile as an aluminum can. But once she pierced through the metal, her head became stuck inside.

I slammed on the gas, taking her with me. The woman tried to keep up, running along the side of the car while attempting to break free. The car sped up, plowing through the hallway. Her scarf fell from her neck and I saw the tiny frightened doll face on her neck, shrieking louder than the engine.

"I'm sorry it didn't work out," I told the woman. "But you're not the marrying type."

The driveway ended up ahead with a wooden wall blocking the path. I strapped on my safety belt and braced myself. When the car burst through the wood, the woman's head was ripped from her body. Violet blood sprayed across the side of the vehicle and the metal hammerhead dropped into the backseat. Although the woman's face and neck had been ripped away with the rest of her body, a stainless steel spinal column was still attached to the hammer, covered in webby fluids and blue tendons.

It took a few moments to realize I was no longer in the mansion. I was on the road. The real road. Driving beneath the night sky.

I stuck my head out of the window and howled at the moonlight.

"I did it," I said, banging on the steering wheel. "I actually got out of there…"

Hitting the gas, I sped down the country highway. I wanted

to get out of rural Oregon as soon as fucking possible.

Looking in the rearview mirror, I saw something coming up behind me. It looked like a storm cloud moving in quickly, blocking out the moonlight on the horizon.

"What kind of storm is that?"

It wasn't actually a storm coming up behind me. It was more like a tornado—a tornado of construction.

"You've got to be kidding me…"

As fast as lightning, the hammer wives were building a tunnel over the street. They built it faster than I could drive. Like a snake traveling through the country, the tunnel grew across the earth. I couldn't even see the hammer women working as they constructed the building, just eight blurry forms buzzing across the edges of the walls. I couldn't even figure out where all the wood and nails were coming from.

I pushed the gas as far as it could go, but the car just wasn't fast enough to escape them.

"God damn you Toyota Corolla," I yelled at the car. "The slowest goddamn machine on the planet!"

The moonlight disappeared and I was covered in darkness as the hammer women passed over me, swallowing me within their tunnel. But I continued driving. There was still an opening up ahead.

There was no sign of an end to the tunnel, but I kept driving. Half an hour passed. I could tell the tunnel was curving. The street below my tires was now made of wood. The hammer wives had me. The road was curving back toward their mansion. There was no escape.

The next thing I knew I was back where I started. The tunnel went straight into the mansion, through the hallways, and the engine stalled out as it reached the heart of the building. I found myself parked in the dining room where I had signed my contract. The hammer wives sat around the table, as if waiting for me. One of their chairs was empty. Another was occupied by the hammer woman with broken legs.

I sat in the car, just staring at them and shaking my head.

"Fine," I said. "I'm through running."

I stepped out of the vehicle and opened the door to the backseat to arm myself with the only possible weapon I could use—the severed head of their fallen sister.

"I'll take down each and every one of you if I have to," I said.

Holding the massive hammerhead out to the side, I gripped the metal spinal cord and twirled it in a circle, as if it were a ball and chain.

"Who's next?" I said.

The women stared at their sister's severed head in my hands. All but the crippled one stood from their seats.

"I could never love you," I told them. "How could I? You're grotesque inhuman monsters. You're living abominations. Who could ever love you?"

One of the women stepped forward. She removed the scarf from her neck, revealing her tiny doll face.

"This was never about love," said the woman in a high squeaky voice.

My eyes widened with shock when I heard her speak. I had no idea the hammer wives could talk. Even my uncle said they couldn't speak with their mouths.

"We just want to break you," she said.

Then she came at me. I hurled the hammerhead at her, but it was too slow. The bloody spinal column slipped through my fingers as the woman's head slammed into my shoulder.

I shrieked as my arm popped out of the socket.

Another woman came at me and slammed me in the chest. My ribs cracked and it felt as though my lungs had flattened against the back of my spine, all of my breath exploding into my sinuses. Upon impact, I flew backward and landed on the hood of the car.

"You bitches," I wheezed, hardly able to speak or breathe.

Then the others came at me. They hammered my arms and feet. They crushed my kneecaps and pounded my flesh like dough. My blood wet the black lips painted on the front of their hammerheads.

It was a sexual experience for them. A bludgeoning orgy. They removed their clothing and my blood painted their nude flesh as they gently, sweetly broke my bones.

They awoke my swollen tongue-like organs and feasted upon the milky fluids. All of them drank from me at once, piling on top of me, slurping the fleshy tubes like ravenous hammer-shaped vampires trying to suck me dry.

When they were finished, they lifted me from the hood of the car and took me deeper into the mansion. They dragged me past cages of alien rodents and aquariums of furry fish. They carried me down stairwell after stairwell, my mind drifting in and out of consciousness.

I awoke in a subterranean world at the edge of an enormous black lake. Candelabras lined the waterside. The hammer wives were in black wedding dresses.

"What is this?" I asked, my voice weak and scratchy from a broken voice box.

The wife who spoke earlier was standing to my right, holding me in place.

"You will now marry us properly," she said. "In the eyes of our gods."

And just as her words were spoken, bubbles foamed across the surface of the vast underground lake. Then up from the ancient murky depths, my new gods arose to greet me.

LEMON
KNIVES 'N'
COCKROACHES

We are spider-crawling through the dark places between the walls like maggots under dead skin. Boney limbs and hooks on our fingertips to help us slither through the tight pathways.

Alyxa and all of her dirty smells ahead of me, her cricket legs creeping the crawlspace, greases scraping off of her and coating the walls as she moves, leaving a path for me to follow. Every time she spreads her legs to move, a rotten stench attacks me in the face, makes my eyes water, almost collapsing me from my position.

One of the boys is following behind, Paul I think his name is, not sure. All of the school boys look alike now with their black-painted bodies, bald heads, goggles over their eyes. They don't really speak anymore, driven mindless, inhuman. The boy crawls like a cockroach behind me, overlapping my limbs if my pace slows, cutting into my leg flesh when he misses the wall.

Alyxa stops, freezes in a position with her legs apart to brace herself. Her smell sweeps over me and I try not to breathe, even when breathing through my mouth I can taste the thick scent of her filth. She turns to us and opens her lips to release two lemon knives, sharp handmade knives greased with sour acids yellow in color, dropping them into each of her hands. Dirt-crusted teeth and a cat-dry tongue, looks at me deep through my eyes.

"I love you," she whispers, petting my arm with her bare toes.

I continue to hold my breath, my eyes seal themselves shut from the sting of her fumes, she can't see my expressions in the shadows. The cockroach boy tugs on my legs behind me.

"Let's go," she says, and continues on.

I open my eyes and follow, rubber kneecaps helping me through the crawlspace. More cautious now. We're in the dangerous region, where they are most likely to find us. So many have been killed here, so many that were stronger than me, smarter. Alyxa's the only one left worth saving.

We move vertically through the crawlspace now, into a hole in an air vent, shifting to the space over the ceiling of the first story of the facility, beneath the floor of the second story. And pause, balancing ourselves on the framework so that we do not fall through.

My leg slips and clanks into the frame. That was sloppy. Alyxa puts a metal hooknail to my lips, *hussshhh*, and points down to the vent at our knees.

I nod and slowly pull the vent away, a rush of musty pungent odor surges into the crawlspace, even more rancid than Alyxa's dirty smells. I hand the vent to the cockroach boy who in turn hands me a wire-rope tied in a noose. The opening leads to a deep blackness. I can't see all the way to the ground. A cloth over my nose as I focus on them.

"There they are," Alyxa whispers, but she doesn't have to say anything. They are right below us, like they were waiting for us. They peel open their decayed leathery lips and release deep hungry moans.

I can only see parts of them in the shadows, their cold faces glowing in the dim moonlight from a half-boarded window somewhere down the hallway. No clue how many there are. Their moans are echoing in such a way that it sounds like hundreds. But those are just echoes. Have to be…

"Lower the rope," Alyxa says, and I slide it into the pool of dark as the cockroach boy ties the other end to the metal framework.

"It's just like fishing," she says.

She knows I've never done this before, that I was lying when I said that I was the fisher on the runs that I used to go on with her brother. Back when there were enough people to spread out the runs evenly, so that everyone only had to go on one run every eight days. As of yesterday, we go every other day.

I wiggle the rope slowly at their heads, waving it at them.

Alyxa sighs hard at me, sniff-shaking her head. I'm used to having the cockroach boy's job, hiding in the back, in the safe place.

One of them snatches onto my noose, tugs violently at it, tries to pull me down to him. The noose slips tight around its fingers. "Pull," Alyxa screams and I tug the wire-rope, the creature tumbles from its feet and the wire goes limp.

"Did it break?" my words slurred. My nerves feel like ants crawling up my neck.

"No, it slid from his hand." Alyxa fingers my waist like it's a pat on the back.

We reclaim the rope and retie the noose, lowering it back into the pit of living death. The moaning grows louder as more of them enter the hallway, this kind of commotion brings them all out of hiding.

"Hurry up," Alyxa says. "We can't afford to attract any more of them."

"You think I don't know that?"

Before she can respond a groan pops out of my lungs, my breath is knocked out of me as one of the creatures snatches the wire-rope and rips it from my grip.

"Watch it," Alyxa cries as the rope slashes around at us, the monster below convulsing against the cord, throwing my balance.

I seize the wire-rope and pull, the noose hooking tight around the creature's arm.

"Come on," Alyxa shrieks into my ear. "Pull, pull!"

All three of us reel in the wire, the cockroach boy uses the framework as leverage.

"It's a big one!" I say, as if it really is a fish. "Will it fit through the walls?"

Alyxa doesn't answer, concentrating, the lemon knives propped in her mouth.

The creature comes into focus: a very large corpse, white and naked, its skin wrinkled with rot. It growls as we pull it in, swinging at us with its free arm.

Just a few inches away from us, we stop pulling. The boy wraps the excess wire-rope to the frame and Alyxa releases her portion, slipping the lemon knives from her lips.

"Okay," Alyxa sighs, leering down at the living corpse at her feet, a hazy film over its eyes. "Are we ready?"

But before we can respond, the dead man grabs hold of the edge of the opening with its free hand and pulls himself up into the crawlspace.

I scream, jerking back away from the zombie, kicking to move, hitting Alyxa in the ankle and she drops one of the knives. I shove myself into the cockroach boy who slips from the framework, falls back and drops through the ceiling.

He quietly disappears into the darkness below.

Alyxa retrieves her lemon knife and stabs both of them through the sides of the zombie's head, their tips touching each other in the middle of the dead man's mind.

She pulls his corpse away from me as I lie there, staring at the quiet hole where the cockroach boy was situated. He went without a scream or complaint, just dropped into the mass of living dead underneath.

"Are you going to drain him?" I ask.

"No time," she says. "We're taking him as he is. Just don't get any blood on you."

Through crawlspaces back to our home, the only room hidden from the undead, deep inside of the walls of the facility, brightened by fire light. We shove the large fleshy corpse through the tight spaces as quick as we can. This one is hardly able to fit, but we grease him up with the oils built up in our scalps and privates to ease him through.

"Don't look at me," I tell Alyxa as she pets my cheek. "Don't touch me."

Upon arrival, several cockroach boys rip the body from our arms and immediately string it upside-down from the ceiling, poke holes into its neck and wrists with bones carved into knives, bleeding it into a large saucer.

"Ahh, dinner is here," says a scratchy voice behind me. "And a very good piece of meat I see."

The voice forms into the shape of a man as he steps out of the shadows and into the fire light.

"Everything went perfect then, I see."

"Not exactly," we tell him.

"What do you mean, *not exactly?*"

"I'm sorry, Thomas…" I say. "We lost the boy."

The man's eyes droop from their lids, and his mouth shivers. He lets out a shriek and falls to his chubby knees, covering his face to cry. "No, not Charlie, anyone but Charlie," he says in his tears. He sounds almost sarcastic.

"He didn't scream," I tell him. "It couldn't have been a painful death."

"Of course he didn't scream," Thomas shrieks at me. "I taught him not to scream, not to give in to pain or fear."

"I'm sorry, Thomas," I say, but the man curls into a fat ball and rocks back and forth.

"Come warm me," the man says to the cockroach boys draining the corpse, and they stop their work to huddle around him, pressing their sickly forms against his fleshy breasts, gurgling.

I step away from them, into the cold shadows to Alyxa who drinks from the drippy pipes. The corners of the room are littered with sick dying children and an old woman.

Alyxa kneels to the old woman.

"Take the blanket off," the woman begs with a leechy voice, her head swaying from side to side. And Alyxa removes the blankets, rubs the places where her arms and legs used to be, the stumps still scabbed and infected.

"Thank you," says the woman. Alyxa smiles.

The woman's name is Mrs. Boontide. I don't know if she

has a first name. Her husband was killed by Thomas several months ago, for breaking his rules. Thomas was always looking for an excuse to kill and eat the elderly. Mrs. Boontide is the last. For having an unruly husband, Thomas has been taking her limbs from her one at a time. Cutting them off and feeding them to his children.

The cockroach boys will do anything he tells them to do. They aren't human anymore. Just empty shells. Insects. He commands them like an army. Faceless, soulless soldiers.

I can hear Thomas whispering to the boys: "Oh, Charlie and I were so close, so friendly. I can't believe he's gone. He was the only *man* here, you know? Now I have to wait for one of you to become a man. Who is the oldest? Paul? You will be a man in almost a year, won't you? That's not very long at all. You can be the new captain of the swim team. Oh, thank God I have you, Paul. Thank you God."

"Why don't you sleep with me anymore?" Alyxa asks me.

We are sitting on a ledge in the elevator shaft, a candle between us, far away from Thomas and his cockroach boys, our feet dangling into the darkness.

"I mean you never even sleep next to me, let alone fuck me," she continues. "Why can't you be affectionate? You say you love me but won't lay a finger on me."

"I don't feel like it anymore," I tell her.

"You don't feel like making love with me?" she says. "You're the one who said the only thing left worth living for is sex, you told me that living in the walls is passionate, our flesh trapped closely together."

"I do love you, Alyxa," I tell her. "And the only reason I don't kill myself right now is because I want to be with you. I'm just bored with it, it's all we've been doing for the past three years. All day, every day. And I can't handle all those abortions.

You say it provides food for us, but I just can't deal with it anymore."

"It's safer than eating the dead," Alyxa says. "I can't help but wonder if I'm going to catch the disease every time I take a bite of their flesh. With the abortions, I can actually eat without worries. The idea that I'm eating my babies doesn't even bother me anymore. It seems almost natural."

"*Our* babies," I tell her.

"I don't know why you refuse to eat them."

She doesn't see my head shaking at her in the dark.

I let her screw me in the elevator shaft, digging her nails deep into my chest. Her dirty smells encase my body, cut into me like razors. I try not to breathe through my nose or mouth, trying to inhale through my eyes, ears, pores on the skin...

"Do you remember what the light looks like, what the sun looks like?" I ask Alyxa, her greasy head lying in my armpit.

"I don't remember these things."

"Sometimes I want to take a chance and go to the roof. Just to see the sun again."

"There's no sun anymore," Alyxa tells me, her eyes shifting to mine, glistening in the dark. "It disappeared when the dead came out of their graves."

"We don't know that for sure."

"It might as well be true," she says, kissing my gritty hand and licking some sweat away.

The dead man hanging from the ceiling has lost most of his meat. All the cockroach boys scrabbling his flesh into their throats, their only form of communication being growls and snorts. Thomas says there isn't enough food to go around, so

Alyxa and I have to go searching for beetles and rats. It's an exhausting job with little reward, but we like the idea of leaving the company of our twisted leader, escape into the walls.

"Is it time to kill ourselves yet?" Alyxa asks me.

"Not yet," I say. "I won't die until I see the daylight again."

"It's a sweet dream, but we both know it will never happen."

"It will happen," I tell her. "Some day."

She wraps her sweaty palm around my mouth and licks my ear.

"Let's kill ourselves now," she says. "Let's feed the zombies."

"Not yet," I say.

"Let's become zombies together," she says, a chuckling whisper. "Let's be undead flesh-eating corpses." Then a slitting sound close to my eardrum.

I scream in pain, blood gushes from the side of my head. I jerk to look at her, she's holding a lemon knife in one hand and my ear in the other.

"I'm a zombie," she says, folding the ear into her mouth and chewing.

I can hardly breathe from shock. She swallows my ear, licking her lips at me.

And she's just playing a game...

"I'm going to eat you," she screams out. "Let me taste more of you."

I stagger, holding the blood inside of my head.

"Get away," I scream.

She cuts me across the shoulder. I shriek, scrambling back, trying to get away. No room for agility when between the walls, especially for a man.

"Let me eat you," she screams. "I'll fuck you and eat you at the same time."

I lunge at her, grab her knife and bite her ear. My molars grind against it and tear it off, nearly choke on it. Blood rivers down her shoulder and her eyes widen. She howls at me, breaks free from my hold. I feel the blade enter my muscle and loose skin, cutting my arms and legs. Alyxa drops the knife, licking the blood, drinking pieces of my flesh into her mouth and chewing it free.

She sucks her severed ear from my lips and gulps, licking my forehead and laughing at herself.

"I'm never going to die," she tells me. "Help me die."

Thomas is becoming more insane every day. He has started painting murals on the walls with a young boy's shit. We have to go onto our elevator ledge to escape the smell. Our heads and my limbs all bandaged with a dead cockroach boy's clothes. Alyxa becomes more and more ready to commit suicide, excited for it, depressed when she realizes she is not yet dead.

"Want to try getting to the parking lot?" I ask Alyxa and she smiles. "I don't want to die until I see daylight. I was thinking... maybe we should try to make it outside. Steal a car. You know, see how far we can get."

"There's no chance we can make it out of the building. We've tried before, remember?"

"That was years ago. There aren't as many of them as there used to be."

"It sounds good to me…" she says. "But I hope you realize we most likely won't get twenty feet outside these walls. I don't want you to be disappointed if you die before making it outside."

I throw bits of rock down the shaft. "I've thought about it all day long."

Alyxa is jealous when Mrs. Boontide passes away.

She presses her fingers against the woman's dead face and curls the skin into odd expressions, making her look happy or sad or just warped. Playing with her face like silly putty.

"It's weird," she tells me. "It feels fake."

She pulls my hand towards the skin but I resist.

"What's wrong with you?" she asks.

"I just don't want to touch her," I say.

"You'll eat her but you won't touch her skin?"

"I don't see what's so fun about playing with a dead woman's face," I say.

"You're becoming such a bore," she says.

"You're becoming another person," I say.

"When are we going to try the escape?" she asks.

She menstruates onto a plate for the cockroach boys' dinner.

"Later," I say.

"You've been saying that for the past two days," she says.

"I'm not ready yet," I say.

"I'm going to go without you," she says.

"We'll go for it soon," I say. "I promise."

Alyxa flicks at Mrs. Boontide's cheeks and nose.

"I just want us to be dead..." she says.

I pick the maggots out of the old woman's wounds and swallow them without chewing.

"Come here," Thomas screams at Alyxa. "Take your clothes off and come to me."

We are lying in bed, half of the cockroach boys are gone on a run, and Thomas has his wild twisty voice testing our obedience to him.

"Alyxa, my patience is a weak little thread. Come here quickly."

"I'm not going to fuck you," she tells him, calm and stern.

"Get over here!" his voice grinding into the back of his throat.

She stands and drops her clothes, her naked smells forcing me to look in the other direction. By the way she walks to him,

I can tell she has her lemon knives hidden between her legs.

"After all this time, you now want to fuck me."

Thomas laughs. "I'm not going to fuck you," raises an eyebrow. "But Timmy here wants you to fuck him. He's been begging me to make you take his virginity for so long... I just can't refuse him anymore."

Alyxa chuckles. "You're joking."

This is no joke. I stand up.

The other two cockroach boys lunge for me and tackle me to the ground, hard knees in the back of my neck, vision getting dizzy. The hole where my ear used to be opens up and spills blood onto the cement.

"I never joke, Alyxa," Thomas says. "You are a birthday present, from me to him. Please be a nice present and give yourself with a smile."

Thomas grabs hold of her shoulders and pushes her to the skinny boy in the corner. "Are you ready, Timmy? Beautiful little Timmy…"

The boy nods furiously and Alyxa struggles against Thomas.

Trying to hold her still, he says, "If you don't behave yourself, I will have to give presents to all the boys."

"You're sick," she says. "He's just a boy."

"Yes, that's why he wants you. He's going through that phase in his life. Only boys want women."

Alyxa slips to the ground and jerks her eyes at me. She is starting to tear. Thomas has overpowered her arms and she cannot reach the lemon knives she has hidden. I struggle to get off the ground, but the cockroach boys bend my legs and arms back until they hear high-pitched squeals coming from me.

"Your man over there is not really a man," says Thomas. "I thought he was a man a long time ago, when I loved him. I wanted him *so* badly, but he rejected me. Because of you. That's when I realized he wasn't a man at all. Just a boy. No more than any of these teenagers we share the walls with. A little worthless boy. How can a man love a boy? Only *women* love boys."

He pulls my lover's arms, dragging her. "But some boys, like my Timmy and my Paul, have the ability to someday become men. Like caterpillars becoming butterflies."

Thomas stops tugging on Alyxa, pausing to gaze into Timmy's eyes. The boy's goggles shine the fire light back into his leader's smile. They are frozen long enough for Alyxa to pull the lemon knives out of her secret places and stab Thomas in the inside of his leg.

A deep scream and Thomas is thrown to the ground, blood leaking down his legs.

The cockroach boys leap from me and charge Alyxa, I catch one of their ankles, but his foot slips through. They move in silence, drawing sharp blades longer than Alyxa's, raise them high above her and then they pause. They are frozen in mid-strike.

"Don't move," Alyxa says, calmly.

I get up. Move to a better view. A lemon knife is at each of their throats, one of them is partially inside a boy's neck, just a twitch away from the jugular.

Thomas grabs a pipe from Timmy's feet and lifts it like a baseball bat.

"Drop it, Thomas," Alyxa tells him. "Or they'll both die right here in front of you."

"You wouldn't," Thomas puts the pipe down slowly. "They're only children."

"We're all children," Alyxa tells him, inching the blades deeper into their necks.

"Don't, please," Thomas cries.

His body folds into a ball. He screams, "Let them go now!"

"If I let them go they will kill me."

"If you kill them you will die, I promise you."

"It sounds like it's worth the risk." Alyxa smiles at the young men, their eyes jiggling in their goggles.

"Alyxa…" I say, taking the blades away from the boys. "Don't do it. We can try to escape now. We'll see the sunlight."

I smile at her, but she will not look at me.

As if shrugging, Alyxa turns away from them to look at Timmy.

"Happy birthday," she tells him, smiling.

Then a slicing sound and blood sprays into musty air, the two cockroach boys holding their wide-open necks as they fall to the ground. Redness pools under our bare feet.

And she just stares at Thomas coldly. Her eyeballs are black pools without any white in them.

The shock has taken the breath out of Thomas. "You... bitch," he chokes, too weak to cry. "I can't believe... you... killed them. You fuck...ing bitch."

"What did you do?" I yell at her, and her face twitches back at me. "Kill Thomas. He's the only one who deserves to die."

"I'd rather see Thomas suffer."

I gather our things, dressing myself in the correct attire for fighting the living dead, collecting the sharpest homemade weapons.

"Hurry up," I tell Alyxa, throwing the rubber outfit at her. "We need to go before the others get back."

"What about Thomas?" she asks.

I look down on the pathetic wretch, his face wrinkled downwards. "Kill him, quickly."

"No, I want him to come with us." She laughs, cutting her own shoulder with a lemon knife.

"No time for games," I tell her. "He's just going to slow us down."

"I won't rest until I make this perverted asshole suffer," she tells me, bringing her knife to his chin. "Either I stay here and do it or I feed him to the dead."

"Fine, take him," I tell her.

And she runs up to me and licks all the blood off the side of my head.

Last week, Alyxa was lying next to me in the darkness. She was cradling her stomach as if pregnant again. It was too dark to see, but I swear I could hear her smiling, her eyes closed just smiling at the thoughts that were spinning around in her head.

"Do you remember when mom used to make pies in the summer?" she asked me.

"My mom never made pies," I told her.

"She made them on Saturday afternoons when the sun was directly above us," her voice like a little girl's. "The sun was so big, warming up the garden in the backyard, hugging flavor into mom's pies through the window."

"I thought you hated the sun?"

"No, not before mom died," she told me. "It was big and warm and comforting, just like my mom. And I'd play in the sunshine all day long, squishing frogs into jelly and rubbing it on the sidewalk to cook."

"Yes, of course," I say.

But she's never known her mom...

We leave the sick people behind. Most of them only have a few days left anyway. The very young cockroach boys hide behind the skeleton piles, waiting for us to leave so they can eat the two freshly dead teenagers.

Thomas doesn't put up a fight as we push him through the crawlspaces, but he's so fat that he can hardly get through. Fat from eating people.

"Let's not go down through the ceiling," I say. "They'll be expecting us there."

"Where then?" Alyxa asks.

"One of the office vents," I say.

"But those are farther from the exit," she says.

"But they won't be waiting for us there," I say.

She nods.

I was right. Peering through a vent into one of the stale offices, there aren't any corpses in sight. Unfortunately, the vent is screwed shut. We'll have to break through and the noise will probably attract them into the room.

The door to the office is shut. It might even be locked. That helps a little, but we don't want them to swarm in the hallway outside the door. We'd never be able to get through them that way.

Alyxa kicks the vent in. The bang echoes through the room but we don't hear any noises in response.

"Come on," she says, sliding through the opening.

She pulls Thomas's plump legs and I push on his shoulders with my feet until he can get through the vent hole. He cries out as his flesh compacts. His breaths heavy, like he's suffocating. He hasn't gone through enough of the crawlspaces to get over the claustrophobia.

This attracts the dead. I can hear them in the next office, pounding on the walls to get through.

"Hurry up," Alyxa cries.

I shove all my weight into Thomas, not worried if I hurt him or break his neck in the process. Let out all my anger to get him through.

He plops out on the other side, lands on his legs weird.

"Get up," Alyxa tells him, but he won't get to his feet.

I crawl out of the shaft and hurry to the door. No sounds when I put my ear to it, but the scratching against the other wall might be interfering.

"Leave him," I say.

"But I want to watch him die…"

"Come on," I say.

She pulls Thomas up by the hair. His ankle must have been twisted because he can't stand on it anymore.

"You don't want to do this," Thomas cries. "We'll die horribly."

"As long as I get to see you die first," she says.

Out in the hallway, the corpses are animated mannequins. Naked, mechanical, featureless. Spread out but not close enough to be a problem yet.

Alyxa and I drag the fat man across the tile floor, over rubble and mummified body parts scattered around like old laundry.

"We've got to run," I say. "Drop him."

"Not yet," she says. "I want to feed him to them."

The fat man oozes a yellow substance from his mouth.

"You…" he chokes on the goop in his throat. "I'll kill…"

He falls to his knees and pukes up a blanket of yellow muck. Alyxa pulls on him to get up, but he's glued to the floor. The regurgitation becomes violent. Yellow squirts from his nostrils, through the corners of his eyes.

"What's wrong with him?" I ask.

Snails crawl through the soup. They stick to Thomas's hands, to the sides of his face. A slug stretches out of his nostril and dribbles grease onto his upper lip.

"Help me," Alyxa says.

I grab Thomas by the other shoulder and we lift him off of his knees, but he jerks out of our grasp and stabs me in the chest.

We let him go and he backs away, pointing a knife at us. I look down at my chest: a little round hole. Black blood squirts out of it with a swirl of mucus.

It's not a knife, it's a pen. But he holds it like a knife, threatens us to back off.

"Murderers!" he cries, snails and slime still pouring out of his mouth. A thick yellow waterfall pooling onto his belly.

Alyxa curls her eyebrows at the undead.

"Eat him!" she cries. "You're too slow!"

The closer the corpses get, the slower they seem to move.

She runs up to the zombies and smacks them in the face, gets behind them and shoves them at Thomas. They don't attack her. They just groan at her through holes in their skulls.

"Come on! Eat him!" she cries.

Thomas just points his pen at me, holding his mouth shut with his other hand, snot dripping through his fingers.

"I'll eat him then!" she cries.

Thomas turns to point his pen at her as she leaps onto him, grabs him around the shoulders and wraps her legs around his waist. He stabs at her with the pen but it does not break the skin.

Alyxa bites into his neck and chews through his flesh until she opens a major blood vessel. But instead of blood gushing out of him, it is the same yellow snot that he has been regurgitating. It leaks down Alyxa's lips and chest. She growls at him, a flesh-hungry ghoul.

He falls to the floor and seizures. Alyxa squeezed around him like a spider, trying to hold down his flapping limbs as she eats him.

The living dead pass me and pile on top of Thomas. They tear him apart, taking pieces of him into their black mouths. But they don't attack Alyxa. They eat with her, like she is one of them.

"Come on," she says to me with yellow slop all over her face. "Join us."

I back away from them, holding the blood in my chest by plugging the hole with my little finger, and she returns to feasting on the fat man.

The living dead do not attack me either for some reason. They bump me out of their way to get to Thomas. I stagger down the hallway, looking for a room to duck into.

A hand grabs me.

"Come back," she says. "We're safe."

She digs her fingers into her crotch and rubs it on my face. I cough at her.

"It smells like death," she says. "That's why they aren't attacking us. The menstrual blood stains on our bodies have turned rancid. They think we're dead like them."

She rubs more rotten smells onto my neck and stomach. I hold my nose and mouth but still feel like puking.

"Let's go," she says, smiling, kissing me on the forehead.

But instead of taking me towards the exit, she goes back to Thomas's body to eat more of him.

"What are you doing?" I whisper.

"I want to feed," she says.

"We've got to get out of here," I say.

"No," she says, "we don't have to leave anymore. We can fit in with the living dead now. We can live with them."

"We must leave," I say.

"We'll never leave," she says.

And she goes back to Thomas.

She drops her weight next to the gurgling zombies, but her knees don't hit the ground. A wire has hooked her by the neck. She opens her eyes wide at me as the noose tightens around her throat.

"Alyxa..."

She doesn't have the air to cry out as the wire pulls her off of her feet, staring at me with baby eyes and kicking her legs. I see the cockroach boys up in the ceiling, their minds as dead as the zombies behind those black goggles. They don't realize Alyxa is not one of the zombies as they reel her in, lift her up into the ceiling and stab her in the head with a lemon knife.

They bleed her like a cow, then fold her limp body under their arms and pull her with them deep into the crawlspace.

I lie down in the puddle of Alyxa's blood and press my face against the floor to feel the last of her warmth, rubbing my arms in it like I'm making a snow angel.

Staggering through the halls like I'm one of the corpses, blood no longer gushing from the hole in my chest, looking for a way out. Hours pass. I can't find an exit anywhere. The hallways seem to go for miles in every direction. After a day, I camp out in an office, eat a spider and the contents of its web, then continue to search for a way into the street. I have to see the sun one more time before I die.

Days go by. Still nothing but corridors and empty rooms crowded with the living dead.

They look at me as if I'm one of their own. Just another walking corpse that refuses to die. And I'm beginning to look at myself in the same way.

WAR
PIG

The crowd went crazy as the pig-man slammed into the bars of the cage and dropped to the concrete floor. Blood gushed from his gnarled snout, his massive frame twitching as his eyes rolled back into their greasy sockets. The colossal bear-man hovered above him and roared at the audience, beating his furry chest with big black paws. They cheered for him like no other fighter I have ever seen before.

At that moment, I thought it was the end. The War Pig had finally been defeated. This didn't come as much of a shock to me. His opponent, Grizzly Titan, was larger, younger, fiercer. And he was a fucking bear. Even though the old pig had been the longest running champion in the history of the fights, he had no chance against a grizzly bear. Still, I hoped against reason that he would have found a way to beat him. After all, this is a fight to the death. And he is my father.

War Pig snorted and drooled as Grizzly lifted him by his portly neck and bit into his shoulder. War Pig cried out, a human cry, as the bear growled and thrashed at his flesh. The cry was the only thing I still recognized about my father.

The bell rang before Grizzly Titan could rip my father's throat out. At first, I was relieved. But then I thought it would have been better if he had just finished him off then and there, rather than dragging out the inevitable.

The bear spit War Pig out of his mouth and pushed him back to the ground. Then he stomped at the guard to let him out of the cage. There would be an hour break before the next round, but the old pig spent the first ten minutes of it just lying on the floor, holding the blood in his gaping wounds. Eventually, the doctor's aides scraped him up into a stretcher and carried him out of the cage into the back of the factory.

I wasn't excited to go see the old man. I was done saying goodbye to him a long time ago, and I wasn't willing to do it again just because it was for real this time. But still, if I was going to get any money for lunch today (or any day in the future) I knew I had better get it from him then.

The lower deck of the factory was all standing room. This was where the commoners, the wannabe fighters, and the families of the fighters got to watch the match. The real crowd watched from the upper deck. I had never been allowed up there before.

I pushed my way through the filthy dog shit-smelling mob, knocking a hyena boy off balance. He growled at me, but it only made me laugh. The kid was only fifteen and was already on the serum. Younger and younger people were taking it these days, in the hope that it would get them out of the ghetto. That was what my dad thought when he first took it, but we still lived in squalor. All it did was make him into a hideous creature that killed other creatures for the amusement of the upper class.

They called it the lycanthrope serum, or L-serum. For a member of the working class, it cost a month's wages for each shot unless you had a manager to pay for them. Every injection would make you a little less human, and a lot more animal. Which beast you transformed into depended a little on your DNA and a lot on chance. Some fighters became werewolves, some became lions, some became mice. My dad became a wild boar. Once you took the shot, there was no going back. The effect was permanent. It took about six shots before you were strong enough to fight. It took about twelve shots before you lost all of your humanity. My dad was on his eleventh shot.

In the locker room, War Pig was sprawled across a large metal table stained with the blood of a hundred different breeds of lycanthrope. He was getting sewn up by a bald doctor who had two extra pairs of mechanical limbs powered by a rumbling engine strapped to his back. The doctor was tall, about my size, but compared to my father's mass he was a mere toddler operating on a giant. The old pig was conscious now, swatting at the puffs of smoke that issued from the doctor's shoulder pipes.

I locked eyes with my father from the doorway, but I didn't approach. His manager, Mr. Crumbly, was beside him, tapping his metal fingers against the wall and glaring up at his ruined prize fighter.

"You need to take another L-shot," said Mr. Crumbly with curly white lips.

"I'm done," grunted my father. "You told me I didn't have to take anymore shots."

As I entered the room, a guard stepped into my path, a soldier who was more machine than human with metal plates for skin, clockwork organs, and a Gatling gun for a left arm. Mr. Crumbly whistled at the guard to let me through, but instead of approaching them I went to a bench on the other side of the room.

"If you don't take another shot then you have no chance," said Mr. Crumbly. "You will lose. You will die."

"My brain won't be human anymore with another shot," said the old pig.

"Your brain won't be anything anymore when it's ripped out of your skull by that monster out there."

The pig man snorted as the doctor crawled across his chest like a spider. "I'd rather die still thinking like a human." Mr. Crumbly wiped pig spit from the lapels of his red suit. "I'll cut you a deal. Take the shot and beat this guy. If you win, I'll let you retire. I'll triple your payout and you never have to fight again."

"Bullshit. You've promised that before."

Crumbly lit a cigar and shook his head. "Fine. Have it your way." He walked a few steps away from him, and then turned back. "But with you dead I'll need to find another fighter. One just like you, but younger and healthier. Know anyone like that?"

Mr. Crumbly glanced over at me, then at the pig man. It took a minute for my father to understand what was meant, but once he did he became furious. He struggled upright and roared at his manager, slapping the doctor off of him and pounding his fist through the back wall. The guard jumped between my father and his manager, ready to turn the crank on his Gatling gun.

"He's eighteen now," said Crumbly. "Perfect fighting age if we can get enough shots in him."

"I'll fucking kill you if you try," screamed the War Pig.

Mr. Crumbly was calm, but backed further away from the operating table. "Take the shot, win the fight, and I won't need another fighter."

My father looked at me. His eyes red. Snot dripping from his snout.

"I'll take it," he said. "But don't you ever fucking stick that shit in my son or I will rip you limb from limb."

"Fair enough." Mr. Crumbly pulled a vial of blue liquid out of his coat pocket and tossed it to the doctor. "Just make sure you win." Then he left the room.

As the doctor filled a syringe with the blue fluid, my father stared at me. We hadn't had much of a relationship in the past few years, mostly because he was so ashamed of what he had become.

"Take the money out of my locker and buy yourself something to eat," he told me. "Take all of it."

I didn't hesitate.

"Buy a train ticket and get out of town," he said.

I frowned at him.

"Even if I wanted to, where would I go?" I asked.

"As far away from here as you can get," he said.

The doctor held up the shot to my father. The pig man nodded back at him. Then the needle went into his blubbery, hairy arm.

"Tommy..." he said, as I was leaving the room. "I don't want you to end up like me."

But I didn't look back.

Through the door, I could hear the sound of his flesh twisting and mutating behind his pig-like screams.

Through the dark and smoky lower deck of the factory, I made my way to a vendor selling balls of hamburger meat on a stick. After paying, I went to the nearby fire pit to cook the meat, passing a rat woman nibbling on her meat raw. The animal people often preferred the taste of raw meat, though they usually ate it that way because using the fire was an extra cost.

While roasting the hamburger balls, I tried not to imagine what my father was going to be like after the shot. I wasn't sure if he would remember how to tie his shoes, remember who I was, or even remember how to speak. It was rare for a fighter to even live long enough to get to their twelfth shot, so I had never seen the effects firsthand.

I was only eight when my father took his first shot. He used to be a butcher until the economy collapsed and he lost his store. Mom died of tuberculosis years before, so it was just the two of us. Everyone knew there was good money in fighting, but back then it was pretty rare for anyone to agree to sacrifice their human DNA for the sake of a little extra cash. But times were getting tougher and tougher, we were living on the streets, and my father would have done anything to put me in a better life.

In the beginning, my father came crawling to Mr. Crumbly.

He knew the man was a ruthless gangster and a flesh peddler, but he thought he had no other choice. Mr. Crumbly took a deep interest in my father. He said that he'd never seen a man more desperate in his life. Mr. Crumbly was a man who profited from desperation.

The next six months were perhaps the happiest time of my life since mom died. My father wasn't fighting yet. He was given a shot a month and during that time our well-being was looked out for. We had a roof over our heads and food on the table. Mr. Crumbly said my father could make it up to him later, by winning some fights.

But at first, I wasn't happy. I didn't know why my father was changing into a pig at the time. I thought he had some kind of disease. It scared me.

"What's happening to you?" I would cry, curled up in a corner.

He smiled at me. "I'm turning into a piggy!" he would say, as if his changes were cute and fun.

He would get down on all fours and wag his butt at me. "Look at my piggy tail! I can wag it!"

His curly tail would make me laugh a little, but it would make me cry a little more.

"Do you want a piggy ride?" he would ask me.

I would shake my head.

"Come on, I know you would like a piggy ride."

I would shake my head.

"I had all these changes done to me just so that I could give you piggy rides, and now you won't even take them?" Then he would give me a pouting sad face, lowering his pig nose at me.

"Okay," I would tell him, to make him feel better.

I would crawl onto his back, hold onto his floppy ears, and he would run around the house making squealing noises until I started laughing. Eventually, I began to like my dad even better as the pig man. He was able to spend much more time with me than he did while working at the butcher shop and he would give me piggy rides whenever I needed cheering up. The more pig-like he got, the more fun he seemed to become.

It went on this way for a few years, until I discovered that he was spending his nights fighting other animal men to the death for money.

"Shots, shots," yelled a dealer passing the fire pit.

I kept my eyes on my food.

"You need an L-shot?" he asked me, peeking through the flames at me. "I got 'em cheap."

"No thanks," I told him.

"Half off," he said.

"No."

He gave me a dirty look and spit on the ground, "Don't you want to be like your old man?" The dealer must have recognized me, but I didn't recognize him.

Even though my meat wasn't fully cooked, I turned and walked away from him, unaware that I was walking into a crowd of dog men. Street gangs commonly hung out in the lower deck of the factory. They came to the fights to buy L and watch the blood fly. Most of them took the serum not to become fighters, but to become stronger more vicious street thugs. If you stayed away from them they usually left you alone, but that dealer had caught me off guard and I wasn't paying attention to where I was going.

A bulldog thug saw me and approached with two of his friends, a Doberman in a trench coat and a Dalmatian with an eyepatch.

"I'll take that," the bulldog said to me with intense dog breath, pulling the food out of my hand and pushing me back. The others laughed as their leader ate one of my meatballs.

As they were about to turn away, I charged at the bulldog and punched him in his slobbery jowls. The stocky punk staggered back in shock. That was probably the first time in a long time that anybody had stood up to him. I tried to retrieve my food, but the Doberman grabbed me from behind. The bulldog punched me in the stomach.

"Do you want to die?" said the bulldog, pulling a knife out of his jacket.

Before he could come at me, the bulldog found a Gatling gun pointed in his face. I turned to see the same metal guard from the locker room. Behind him, stood Mr. Crumbly.

He just whistled at the punks, and they took the hint. They let me go and ran off, taking my food with them. Mr. Crumbly walked over to me and wiped the slobber from my suspenders.

"What was that about?" he asked.

"They took my food."

"And you decided to take on the lot of them?" He laughed. "You've got guts, kid. Just like your old man. Why don't you come to the upper deck and let me buy you some lunch? We can watch the next round from there."

"That's okay," I told him. "I can get some more food myself."

"Nonsense," he said. "Come with me."

The upper deck was a completely different world from the dungeon below. I had never seen anything like it. The lighting was bright. Velvet curtains hung from the walls. Floating steam-powered appetizer trays circled from table to table. All of the people were dressed elegantly, even though most of them were criminals and prostitutes.

As we walked through the upper class crowd, I noticed that the majority of the people were full of clicking noises. They were all mechanical. An old man puffed on a pipe with a golden mechanical arm. His wife sat next to him with her chest opened up, exposing clockwork gears and steam. I had heard it was possible for the rich to replace their insides with machines, so that they could live much longer lives, but I had no idea that *most* of them did this.

Mr. Crumbly sat me down at a table next to two blue jellyfish girls.

"Tommy, these are the Stinger Twins," he said, introducing me to the women at the table. Then he said to them, "This is Tommy. He's the champ's kid."

"Wow," one of them said, pulling me between them and wrapping her smooth arm around me. "You're the son of the War Pig!"

The other one said, "War Pig has always been my favorite fighter!"

The two of them had nearly translucent skin and not a hair on their entire bodies. Instead of hair, they had jellyfish tentacles growing down from bell-shaped sacks on their heads, resembling hats. They were obviously prostitutes. It wasn't uncommon for whores to be given the L-serum. Many clients found lycanthrope women to be more exciting than normal women. It was also a way for their pimps to keep them in a life of servitude, because once you started the L-injections you could never go back to a respectable way of life.

"Have a drink," Mr. Crumbly told me, pouring me a glass of fine whiskey. "I'll have them bring us some steaks before the fight starts."

One of the jellyfish girls coiled her tentacles around my shoulder and glared at me with her sweet bulbous eyes.

"Why do they call you the Stinger Twins?" I asked her.

Then a shock entered my neck from her tentacles and she giggled at me.

"That's why," the other one said.

The girl stung me again, flirtatiously.

"They are wild, aren't they?" Mr. Crumbly said, raising his eyebrows.

"Yeah," I said.

The girls rubbed my legs and stung me some more. I was beginning to feel drunk, but I wasn't sure if it was from the whiskey or the jellyfish toxins.

I could see my father entering the cage below. When the crowd saw him standing upright, bigger than he had ever been before, they applauded. They knew he had taken another shot. They knew he was still in this fight.

There wasn't much changed about my father. His muscles were larger and his stamina was increased, but physically he wasn't much different. Mentally, on the other hand, he seemed to be a completely different person. He had a maniacal glare in his eyes. He was hungry for blood. He wasn't my father anymore.

When Grizzly Titan entered the ring, my father didn't even wait for the bell. He just charged his opponent and slammed his fists repeatedly into the beast's snarling jaw. The crowd cheered as War Pig viciously attacked the bear-man. Even though he was still much larger, Grizzly couldn't push the pig away.

The last time my father looked this scary to me was the first time I saw him fight. I was eleven years old, growing more and more curious of where my father was going at night. He said that he was going to work for Mr. Crumbly, but he never told me what he did.

"I make money," he told me. That was all he said.

At first, I thought he meant that he actually printed money for the government, but by eleven I was old enough to know he was keeping his job a secret. So I followed him to work one night, right to this very factory. I snuck into the building through a ventilation duct, emerging into the roaring crowd of the lower deck. I couldn't see what they were all cheering at, so I slipped my way through the mass of people until I got to the front row.

That was when I saw my father in the cage for the first time. Inside of that arena, he was no longer the man who tried to cheer me up with piggy rides. He was the War Pig. With my own eyes, I watched him beat a moose-man to a bloody pulp. After his opponent could no longer move, my father wrapped his arms around the man's antlers and twisted his head off like the cork of a wine bottle. It wasn't just that he killed a man in front of me that I found horrifying. It was that he seemed so thrilled to be doing it, lifting the bloody moose head up in the air, sticking his tongue in and out of his snout at the audience with glee.

My relationship with my father never recovered after that night. I dropped out of school. I started drinking. I beat up on kids smaller than me. I would never hold onto a friendship with anyone for more than a few weeks.

I attended the fights once I was old enough to get in, but I only did that to make sure I got the money if my dad was ever killed. There was a part of me that wanted him to lose, just so that I could be done with him for good.

There was still a part of me that wanted that as I watched the tides change on my father in the cage. The Grizzly Titan had him against the bars, clawing him across the chest. His fresh stitches opened up and drenched his opponent's brown fur, but he continued throwing punches, biting wildly at the air.

"He's the best fighter I've ever had," Mr. Crumbly said to me. "You should be proud."

"I haven't been proud of my father for a long time, Mr. Crumbly."

The old gangster whistled at the jellyfish girl who wasn't paying much attention to me, and she began kissing my ear with slippery blubbery lips.

"Have you ever thought about fighting?" he asked me.

"A little," I said. "But it's not for me. Besides, the old pig would kill me if I even think about taking the serum."

Mr. Crumbly smiled and pulled out a vial of blue liquid. "You can try it right now if you like."

"But my father..."

"You're a grown man now," he told me. "You can make your own decisions. Besides, you and I both know that your father can't possibly win this one."

"But he took the shot…"

"I wanted him to take the shot so that he could go a few more rounds. All these people came here to see a good show, and I didn't want my prize fighter going out so easily."

I looked into the cage to see War Pig staggering backwards with deep claw marks across his skull.

Then I turned back to Crumbly. "Yeah, I figured he couldn't win this one."

"And after he's dead what are you going to do with yourself? Get a job? Good luck finding anyone hiring a lowlife kid." He saw me looking down at my drink. "No offense."

A jellyfish tentacle coiled across my mouth, as if the girl wanted me to suck on it. I wiped it away, but it just coiled around my ear.

"Fighting pays well," he said. "And who knows, you might be good at it. And if you ask me, you really don't have a lot of options in your current situation."

"I don't know," I said.

"Tell you what…" he filled a syringe and placed it on the table in front of me. Then placed a stack of bills next to it. "I'll pay you $1,000 to take this one shot."

"I don't want to become some freakish creature," I said.

The jellyfish girls stung me a few times for saying that, but continued rubbing my arms and thighs.

"One shot will hardly do anything to you," he said. "You'll barely notice a difference. But we will get to see what kind of animal you might become. If you're not going to become anything we can use then you can take the money and leave. It will be enough to get you started on a new life somewhere. If you become something that would make a great fighter, well, then I'll see if I can cut you a good enough deal."

I stared good and hard at that stack of money. It was more than I had ever seen in my life. More than my dad would make for winning ten fights.

The jellyfish girl who really seemed to like me said, "I want to see what you become. Aren't you curious?"

The other one said, "Maybe you'll become a jellyfish like us. If that happens you wouldn't have to fight."

"And we'd let you spend more time with us," the affectionate one said, caressing my right cheek.

"And you'd be $1000 richer," said Mr. Crumbly.

I looked at the shot and the money, then looked up at the affectionate jellyfish girl. She smiled wide and nodded her head eagerly at me.

"Fine, I'll do it," I said.

And before I had the chance to change my mind, one of the jellyfish girls was already pumping me full of the serum.

By the end of the match, both of the beast men were still standing. My father was in worse shape than Grizzly, but both were badly wounded. Neither one of them exited the cage very quickly.

As the serum raced through my veins, my head began to pound. My flesh started to tickle, then itch, then pulse and twist. The changes were more noticeable than Crumbly had stated. My entire body was changing. My fingernails stretched into claws, my skin grew a thin layer of fur, my teeth sharpened against my tongue. When it was over, I stood up and ripped opened my shirt. My entire chest was coated in golden fur with black spots. A small tail was in my pants.

"Congratulations," Mr. Crumbly said. "You're a jaguar. The first I've ever seen."

"You said it would be hardly noticeable," I said. My voice sounded funny with the longer teeth in my mouth.

Crumbly shrugged. "Some people react better to the serum than others."

The affectionate jellyfish girl rubbed her blue fingers down the spots on my chest.

"Preeettty…" she said.

I slithered out of her tentacles and grabbed the stack of cash.

"I'll give you another $1000 for every shot you take," Mr. Crumbly said to me. "And I'll give you double that if you decide to start fighting. People will pay a ton to see a jaguar in action. What do you say?"

"I'll think about it," I said.

"I'll take that as a yes," he said.

I turned and walked away. As I went through the crowd, I noticed that everyone was staring at me. They seemed thrilled by the sight of me.

"A jaguar, ladies and gentlemen!" Mr. Crumbly shouted at the social elite. "The son of War Pig is a goddamned jaguar!"

They clapped as I went down the stairs to the lower deck.

As soon as I arrived at the lower deck, I noticed a change in the crowd. They were all looking at me with a sense of fear and respect. Even the bulldog punk and his gang of street thugs cowered in my presence.

At that moment, part of me wanted to walk out and take a train out of town just as my father had recommended, another part wanted to break down in tears, and a third part wanted to go right back upstairs and accept Mr. Crumbly's offer. But I found myself doing none of those things. Instead, I went to the back of the factory to find my dad.

Inside the locker room, the doctor was re-stitching my father's old wounds, and stitching in several new ones. At the first sight of me, his eyes widened.

"What did you do?" he said. His voice was a collection of slurs and snorts.

"I took a shot," I said.

"That motherfucker lied to me again!" He grunted. "I'm going to kill him!"

"It was my choice," I told him.

His eyes became red.

"How many times have I told you that this isn't what I wanted for you? I did all of this so that you'd have a better life than mine."

"What else was I going to do?" I said. My voice was probably just as foreign to him as his was to me. "You're not going to be around forever. Hell, you probably won't even survive another day. I'm going to have to feed myself somehow."

"Not like this," he said. "You need to get out of town. Tonight. Don't take another shot. It's not too late to get out of this."

Even though his words were human, I could tell he was having difficulty forming them. His mind was just barely hanging on.

"I'm sorry," I said. "But I'm pretty sure I want to take Crumbly's deal. He said he'd pay me $1000 for every shot I take. That's more than he ever paid you."

War Pig snarled at me.

"If you make so much money now then you can give me back the money I gave you."

I held up the small wad of bills he had given me. "This?"

"Give it back," he said.

I threw it at him. "Here." Then I pulled out my large wad of bills, peeled a few off the top and flicked those at him as well. "With interest."

Then I walked toward the door.

"You're no son of mine," he grunted at me.

I looked back. "I am your son. That's the problem."

I left the room and went straight back to the upper deck. I sat down between the jellyfish girls and stared Mr. Crumbly right in the eyes.

"I'll take the deal," I told him.

And the old gangster's smile grew so wide I could see my reflection in his shiny metal teeth.

The match was supposed to have begun already, but my father was nowhere to be seen. If he didn't show up soon, he would be disqualified. This made Mr. Crumbly a bit uneasy, but he tried to keep calm. He whistled at one of the jellyfish girls to sit on his lap. The other girl stayed with me, stroking my jaguar spots.

The crowd was impatient. They didn't want this to be the end of the fight. Nobody would stand for a win without bloodshed.

Then I heard someone chanting my father's name: War Pig. War Pig. War Pig. War Pig.

It was coming from the lower deck. Mr. Crumbly looked down. A large group of people in the lower deck joined in on the chant.

War Pig. War Pig. War Pig. War Pig.

Then the upper class joined in with the chanting. Even Mr. Crumbly and the jellyfish girls.

War Pig. War Pig. War Pig. War Pig.

Standing in the middle of the ring, Grizzly Titan roared at the crowd, pacing in a circle, ready for his opponent. He was the only person not chanting the champion's name. Besides myself.

War Pig. War Pig. War Pig. War Pig.

Suddenly he burst through the doors of the factory, ripping them off their hinges. When the crowd saw him, they fell silent. The War Pig was even larger than before. He was a fifteen foot high behemoth, double his mass of moments ago. He now had large tusks growing out of his snout, looking more like a warthog than a wild boar. Most of the crowd couldn't believe it was him. They had never seen such a massive lycanthrope.

I knew what had happened. Using the last of his money,

the old pig bought every shot of serum he could get and took them all at once. He didn't want to be human anymore. He just wanted to kill.

He was almost too large to fit through the door of the cage as the guard let him inside. Standing there, dwarfing Grizzly Titan, he roared like a steam engine.

The chanting continued: War Pig. War Pig. War Pig.

He peered down at the bear-man, snot dripping from his tusks.

War Pig. War Pig. War Pig.

When the bell rang, Grizzly charged at my father, growling with claws outstretched.

War Pig. War Pig.

The War Pig threw his fist at Grizzly Titan.

War—

And then it was over. After the massive fist connected, Grizzly's head exploded into a mess of gore and furry bits. The crowd silenced as the headless bear-man staggered across the cage before crumbling to the ground. Then the crowd cheered and hollered for War Pig. The social elite gave him a standing ovation.

War Pig. War Pig. War Pig.

But he wasn't finished yet. War Pig roared and slammed through the door of the cage, crushing the guard beneath it. He climbed the bars until he was face to face with the social elite. Face to face with Mr. Crumbly.

The crowd screamed and scattered as the mammoth leapt to the upper deck. The mechanical guard cranked his Gatling gun at my father, but War Pig just lowered his fist down onto him like he was crushing a tin can. He ripped off the guard's left arm, aimed the gun at the crowd, and opened fire.

Cranking the gun with just two fingers, bullets sprayed through the audience, shattering their metal clockwork hearts. Steam and flames exploded from them as they fell to the ground. Mr. Crumbly used the jellyfish girl on his lap as a human shield. The bullets ripped through her blue flesh until she went limp.

111

Mr. Crumbly calmly wiped her translucent goo from the lapels of his red suit. The other jellyfish girl tried to make it to the stairwell, but her fishy mutation made her less balanced than the humans. She tripped over a corpse and her soft squishy body was quickly trampled to death under the weight of heavy machine people.

When he was out of bullets, War Pig grabbed an old mechanical woman and used her as a hammer against the frenzied mass, clobbering three or four of them at a time, stomping on cowering prostitutes, impaling wealthy gangsters with his blood-soaked tusks. The old woman's head and arms were soon severed, her skin peeled back, until she was just a clicking metal club with which he bludgeoned people.

Mr. Crumbly whistled and three of his fighters came up from the lower deck to protect him. A werewolf, a crocodile man, and a werehorse. But all three were quickly pummeled to death.

The wiry gangster looked back at me. "Your pops sure is something else. A fighter all the way to the end."

Then Mr. Crumbly hit a button on his belt buckle. Steam issued out of his feet and filled the floor around us. His body was lifted off of the ground, into the air above me.

He looked down at me. "I'll be in touch, kid. Remember, we've got a deal."

Then Crumbly flew away, smoke shooting out of his feet as he crossed to the other side of the deck.

The War Pig saw him getting away and roared. He raised the elderly woman's mechanical corpse and aimed at his manager. Then he launched her through the air, spinning like a giant boomerang. Mr. Crumbly didn't notice the projectile until it connected with his legs, flipping him upside-down. He soon found himself rocketing downwards.

Mr. Crumbly's neck cracked as his head slammed against the edge of the cage. His steaming rocket shoes spun his lifeless body into a spiral before disappearing into the crowd cowering in the lower decks.

War Pig ignored the small number of surviving audience members, giving them an opening to escape. With his manager dead, there was a look of satisfaction on his face. Now, he was focused on me.

He approached slowly, crushing tables under his massive hooves. The rage was still burning inside his eyes. When he arrived, he towered above me. I was a spotted helpless kitten. As he came down on me, I curled up into a ball and screamed, "Dad, no!"

But he wasn't trying to crush me. He was only kneeling down. He got on all fours and a loud groan rumbled from his fat neck.

Then I noticed his tail was wagging. He looked over at me and I recognized a familiar expression on his face. Although he could no longer speak, in the back of my head I heard him telling me:

"Do you want a piggy ride?"

I cocked my jaguar head at him.

Then he made another facial expression, as if to say, "Come on, I know you would like a piggy ride."

I found myself climbing onto his hairy sweat-drenched back. He squealed and then charged forward. While riding on the back of my mammoth warthog of a father, I couldn't help but laugh. I realized that he had taken all of those extra shots for me. He knew killing Mr. Crumbly was the only chance he had to get me away from this lifestyle.

My father squealed louder and I giggled like a kid again, as he leapt down from the upper deck, galloped through the dark smoky lower deck, and crashed through the factory exit into the bright afternoon sunshine.

The
Man With The
Styrofoam
Brain

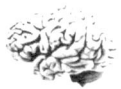

When I died, I knew I was going to hell, but I had no idea I would be going to hell inside the belly of a three-hundred-foot morbidly obese ogre of a demon. After I slit my wrists in the bathtub, an enormous red hand came through my ceiling and ripped my soul right out of my flesh. He picked me up to his face, frowning at me with the jowls of a bulldog and glaring at me with the black ball eyes of a shark.

Like a liquor cabinet, he opened up his torso and revealed an ancient dungeon within the drippy hollows of his body where his liver and intestines should have been. There were rows of man-sized birdcages made of human bones, dangling from black tendons that grew from the ogre's ceiling flesh. He placed me gently inside one of the cages in his belly, as if careful not to damage me in any way before reaching hell. The city lights dimmed around me as the ogre closed the door to his stomach.

The cage swayed as the giant demon continued walking through the city, heading toward his next passenger. As my eyes adjusted to the torchlight emanating from the demon's spinal column, I saw other people in the cages around me. Both of the cells next to me were occupied, one by somebody I quickly named *The Saddest Man in the World*, because there was no other name he could possibly have. The other cage was jam-packed full of people: a young business man and about six Asian women who were gossiping in what I believed to be Cantonese. The man looked miserable to be trapped with the Asian girls, staring out of his bone-cage at me as if begging for help.

After getting stared at for a few minutes, I started to feel uncomfortable and tried to ignore him. I examined the giant's muscled insides, listening to the gurgling sound coming from his bowels far below. The heat of the giant's insides was like that of a sauna. Spiders of sweat crawled down my neck and forehead.

"What did you do?" somebody said.

It was The Man with the Asian Girls.

I looked over at him. "Huh?"

"Why are you going to hell?" he asked. "Did you kill anyone? Or were you a serial rapist or something?"

I shook my head. "I didn't do anything like that."

"You had to have done something."

I rubbed sweat from my face. "Well, I committed suicide, but that's not why I'm going to hell. Last year, I made a pact with a demon."

"You too? You sold your soul to the devil?"

"Yeah."

"Huh. So did I. What did you sell yours for?"

I didn't really want to tell him. "It was stupid."

"Come on, tell me."

"I'd really prefer not talking about it."

"You know what I sold my soul for?" He pointed at the Asian girls around him. "Hot Asian girls." Then he made a gun with his fingers and pointed it at his head. "What a mistake that was. I tell you, never sell your soul to the devil while you're drunk."

"What's wrong with Asian girls?"

"Don't get me wrong, I *love* Asian girls. That's why I asked for them. But I was too drunk to specify exactly what I wanted from the hot Asian girls. All I got was a group of hot Asian girls that followed me around everywhere I went. They hung out in my apartment, eating all of my food, taking over my living room and never letting me use my bedroom or bathroom. They'd hang out in my office at work, they'd chit-chat outside of men's room stalls whenever I was trying to go to the bathroom, they'd gather around me while I was having dinner in restaurants. Keeping jobs and girlfriends was practically impossible. They've been like a plague to me. I couldn't get rid of them. Eventually,

I just couldn't take it anymore and blew my brains out. I knew I'd be going to hell, but at least I'd be free of them."

"But now they're even following you to hell?"

The Man with the Asian Girls sighed. "I'm such an idiot…"

"But being surrounded by beautiful women can't be all bad."

"Yeah, you'd think. But they don't want to have anything to do with me. They always act as if I don't even exist."

"It's still better than what I sold my soul for…"

"What did you sell your soul for?"

I looked away from him, glancing over at the other prisoner. The Saddest Man in the World was just sitting in his cage, examining his hands in his lap. Although he had an absolutely miserable expression on his face, it still didn't seem as if he was too concerned about going to hell.

The Man with the Asian Girls kept looking at me until I said something.

"What about him?" I pointed at The Saddest Man in the World. "Maybe he sold his soul for something as well?"

The Man with the Asian Girls turned to The Saddest Man in the World. "Well, how about you?"

After a moment of silence, The Saddest Man in the World said, "Yeah."

"Yeah, what?" asked The Man with the Asian Girls.

"I sold my soul, too."

More silence. We stared at the miserable man until he spoke.

"I sold my soul to be abducted by aliens," said The Saddest Man in the World.

"What?" The Man with the Asian Girls said, pushing an Asian girl in hot pink shorts out of his way. "Why would you sell your soul for that?"

"I always had a fantasy that I would be abducted by aliens," said The Saddest Man in the World. "I dreamt of being taken up on a ship, brought into the wonderful void of space, and then raped anally over and over again by beautiful alien boys."

An eerie smile cracked the lips of The Saddest Man in the World.

"Umm…" said The Man with the Asian Girls.

"I wanted their tentacles wrapped around me." The Saddest Man in the World closed his eyes and imagined it was happening to him as he spoke. "Suction cups clasped tightly to my breasts, purple tongues sliding up my inner thighs, erect oozing members—"

"Okay, that's enough," The Man with the Asian Girls diverted his eyes as the strange man began to rub his bare nipples.

The Saddest Man in the World continued, "My buttocks spread wide open as their squirming, pulsating—"

"I said that's enough!"

The Saddest Man in the World calmed himself and said, "It was absolutely the best night of my entire life. Totally worth my soul. But ever since then, living on Earth just hasn't been the same. Human beings are just so boring compared to aliens…"

He let out a big sigh and then turned away from us. The Man with the Asian Girls looked at me.

"It's still better than what I sold my soul for," I told him.

The Man with the Asian Girls called up to the people in the cages far above us. All of them had also sold their souls to demons, and each one had sold them for incredibly stupid reasons. There was a guy who sold his soul for front row tickets to a Danzig concert. There was a cheerleader who sold her soul to know what her friends were always saying about her behind her back. There was a woman who sold her soul so that her cute puppy would stay a puppy forever. There was a little boy who sold his soul so that he could speak to ants. But none of them were as stupid as what I sold my soul for.

"So what *did* you sell your soul for?" asked The Man with the Asian Girls.

I shook my head at him. "I really don't want to say."

"How can it possibly be stupider than what everyone else asked for?"

"It is."

"Just give me a hint."

I looked down at the pool of stomach acids below. "Fine .."

"Well?"

I paused. "My girlfriend and I were big cyclists. We didn't have cars, we rode bikes everywhere, as much as we could."

"And?"

"I'm getting to it…" I clenched a fist and then exhaled. "One day, my girlfriend was hit by a car. She went face-first into the windshield. Died right in front of me. Her head was split open. I saw everything. Her brain was like a puddle of pink scrambled eggs. The image horrified me. From that day on, not only was I miserable without the love of my life, but I also was in constant fear that I would break my head open. I stopped riding my bike. I stopped doing anything even remotely dangerous. Brains are such fragile things. I had to be careful not to have anything happen to it. The thought of damaging my brain plagued my every waking moment."

"What did you do?"

"When I met the demon with the devil's contract, I knew I had to ask for something that would ease my worries. I should have asked for invincibility or at least a metal skull, but there was only one thing I could think about. I was thinking that if my brain were made out of another material, something less fragile, something firm and flexible that could absorb impact, then I wouldn't have to worry about damaging my brain anymore. I would be free."

"So what did you sell your soul for?"

I tilted my head to wipe sweat from my ear. My head was so lightweight that it felt almost empty. "I asked the demon to change my brain."

"Into what?"

"Nevermind." I broke eye contact. "It's just too embarrassing to say out loud."

The Man with the Asian Girls groaned loudly and gave up,

rolling his head back against the bars of human bone. Our cages continued rocking back and forth, as the giant demon's feet stomped through town, knocking down trees and crushing dog houses. The demon made just one last stop before he burrowed his way back to hell, picking up an old woman with a crazed smile on her face.

We sat in silence as the giant's hollow torso began to fill with digestive fluids. And just like every miserable day of my miserable life since I sold my soul to that fucking demon, I endured the maddening squeaky sound of blood pumping through my styrofoam brain.

Author's NOTES

SIMPLE MACHINES

In the early days, every bizarro writer had their "metamorphosis" story—where a character awakes one morning to find himself transformed into something different. This is my metamorphosis story. But it's not really about transformation. It's about self-discovery. It's about all the little people inside of you who control who you are and what you do.

Although this is often considered my Kafka tribute, I like to think of it as my tribute to the sketch comedy show *Kids in the Hall*. This is the sketch I would have written had I worked on the show. I would have cast Scott Thompson as Oliver Madu, Mark McKinney as the doctor, Dave Foley with a mustache as his boss, Kevin McDonald as an annoyed co-worker, and Bruce McCulloch wearing drag as the female love interest. Personally, my favorite way to write a short story is to imagine it as a comedy sketch. The first and last stories in this collection were written that way.

This story was originally published in the second issue of *The Magazine of Bizarro Fiction*. I donated this story to the publication to help get it off the ground. I highly recommend checking out some issues if you haven't already. It's constantly amazing, especially compared to the typical small press genre rags that come and go.

RED WORLD

I wrote this novelette when Chuck Palahniuk was my instructor at Clarion West in 2008. There's nothing like getting help on a story from somebody of his caliber. It's kind of mind-blowing. That guy understands the craft in ways that most people have never even thought about before, even other writers at his level. While he is far from a perfect writer and I'm not necessarily the hugest fan of every book he's written, I do believe he's one of the greatest of our time.

I consider *Red World* a major turning point in my writing style. It has been my favorite short story ever since I finished it, mostly because of the way the story unfolds. This method has really altered the way I write books. The focus on backstories that has become prevalent in my work in recent years—such as *Zombies and Shit, Crab Town, Tumor Fruit, Apeshit, Armadillo Fists*, and *Warrior Wolf Women of the Wasteland*—was all because of this story.

I'd like to thank Chuck and the rest of my Clarion class for putting so much effort into helping me evolve as a writer. I'd also like to thank Matthew Humphrey, who published this novelette as a limited edition paperback through his new company White Belly Press and Jeff Burk who published this in *The Magazine of Bizarro Fiction #6*.

HAMMER WIVES

So these days I try to include an unpublished novelette in every collection I release, something that serves as a title story. I did this with *Fantastic Orgy* and then I did it with *Hammer Wives*. Originally, the title story was going to be *Cuddly Holocaust*. But that story ended up being a short novel, far too long to place into a collection. So I had to try again. I succeeded with Hammer Wives. Had I failed I would have tried writing another story I had on deck called *The Boy with the Chainsaw Heart*. It's a story I still might write some day.

There's not much to say about Hammer Wives outside of the fact that I wanted to write a bizarro-style gothic horror complete with eccentric wealthy man inviting estranged family member for dinner at his creepy rustic mansion. There were even some vampire-like creatures involved, but they weren't exactly vampires because they had hammers for heads. Somebody recently asked me if this story was inspired by Hammer Films and I found it strange I never thought about that before. I'm sure it was influenced by the style of Hammer movies yet the word "hammer" wasn't in the title for that reason at all. I guess it could have been a tribute. I used to have a tradition of watching Hammer movies whenever I was sick with the flu and bedridden. Those old horror movies always seemed to cheer me up.

This story was also inspired by the works of Junji Ito. And I guess Lovecraft as well, but I think that's only because Ito was influenced by Lovecraft. In any case, I'm proud of Hammer Wives. It was a fun story to write. It was also strangely sexy—in ways that really should not be considered sexy. I'll never look at hammers (or nipples) the same way again.

LEMON KNIVES 'N' COCKROACHES

The last three stories in this collection were all published in a horror anthology series edited by John Skipp. One anthology had the theme of Zombies, one Werewolves, and one Demons. This story was published in the zombie anthology. It was also the only story that wasn't specifically written for Skipp.

I originally wrote this story in 2001. It was the only short story written by me between 2001 and 2007 besides *Porno in August*. The first anthology I wrote it for was going to have an introduction by George Romero. That's why I wrote this in the first place. I wanted to be published in a book that Romero was introducing. And once this story was accepted I drank myself stupid in celebration. But that book never came out.

Then another zombie anthology picked up this story a few years later, but I had second thoughts once I saw the cover design. It featured a stupid Goosebumps-style mummy on the cover. I couldn't imagine any self-respecting zombie fan would ever buy such a dumb-looking book, so I pulled my story. I don't care if I make much money off of short story sales, but I at least want people to read it. I was sure nobody would ever read a book with such a ridiculous cover. But then, soon after that the zombie boom hit in 2004, the anthology became a huge success, despite the dumb-looking cover. I felt like quite the huge idiot for pulling my story. Serves me right for being such a critical douchebag.

The story was then picked up by the anthology *Aim For the Head*, which went on hiatus for five years until the editor dropped off the face of the planet. This kind of thing happens all the time. I'm pretty used to it. No big deal at all.

Ten years after it was written the story finally saw the light of day in the most definitive zombie anthology to come out since *Book of the Dead* was published in 1989—*Zombies: Encounters with the Hungry Dead*. Edited by the same guy as the Book of the Dead series, John Skipp really knows how to pick them. To me, this was far better than getting published in the Romero-introduced anthology or the successful mummy cover anthology. This was John Fucking Skipp's new zombie anthology. The guy who put splatterpunk literature on the map. The guy whose books taught me how to transcend genre when I was a dorky junior high kid with hopes and dreams. It's an honor to have been published in that anthology, alongside legends of horror Stephen King, Ray Bradbury, Neil Gaiman, Robert McCammon, and Joe Landsdale.

WAR PIG

After the success of *Zombies: Encounters with the Hungry Dead*, John Skipp asked me for another story to go into his next anthology, *Werewolves and Shapeshifters: Encounters with the Beasts Within*. The first thing I submitted was a novella set in my Warrior Wolf Women universe called Barbarian Beast Babes of the Badlands. I figured if I were going to write a werewolf story it should somehow connect to my werewolf novel. Unfortunately, it was far too long and ridiculous. He was also full of werewolf stories and wanted fiction with other types of shapeshifters. So I wrote another story called *War Pig*. I pitched this story as a steampunk verison of *Fight Club* with werepigs. That concept sold me immediately before I even wrote it. And it also sold the editor. Although it's not exactly the concept I pitched—I doubt it could be considered steampunk at all—I'm incredibly happy with how the story turned out. I consider it my most successful short story next to *Porno in August* and *Red World*.

Author Jeremy Robert Johnson gave me shit for the title, because… Well, you can guess why anyone would give me shit for that title. But I like it. Now that I think about it, Jeremy probably just wished I called it *War Pug*. He is a big pug enthusiast after all. It would have been about a Pug Viking that bites ankles and pillages a living room while high on the lightning mead of Thor.

THE MAN WITH THE STYROFOAM BRAIN

This was written for the third Skipp anthology called *Demons: Encounters with the Devil and His Minions*. It was published under the title "Stupid Fucking Reason to Sell Your Soul." The title was changed because the editor and publisher thought my title gave away the ending. I was okay with the change at the time, but I decided to go back to the original title for this collection. I liked it too much. In fact, the whole reason I wrote the story in the first place was because of the title.

This was such a short story because the editor needed a piece of flash fiction. He wanted something very weird and very short. This was what I delivered. Originally, I had two ideas for demon stories that I was going to write for this anthology, but they ended up far too long. In fact, the first story was *I Knocked Up Satan's Daughter* which was published as a novel in 2011. Then there was *Fantastic Orgy*, which was the title novelette of my last collection.

Coming up with stories for these Skipp anthologies has resulted in many projects. His fourth anthology, *Psychos: Serial Killers, Depraved Madmen, and the Criminally Insane*, was the first one not to include a story by me. But I did start a story which has been turned into a short novel called *As She Stabbed Him Gently in the Face*. Writing for Skipp has helped me produce even more than usual and it's been a hell of a lot of fun. I need to buy that man a taco one day.

BONUS SECTION

This is the part of the book where the author tosses in a few pages of half-assed filler to make up for the fact that his collection is only six stories long.

Writing six was hard enough!

Thank you for reading my new short story collection, *Hammer Wives.*

It's me CM3!

They say nobody really buys story collections anymore, but since you're reading this right now it means you've bought it. That makes you DOUBLE AWESOME

For being DOUBLE AWESOME, I'm going to give you the double awesome reward of taco education.

Taco education is where I teach you about the wonders of designing and eating tacos.

Shall we begin?

If you're planning to design tacos you should remember that there are only two kinds of tacos to choose frcm...

CARNE ASADA
SAUERKRAUT

AND   ITALIAN
MEATBALL

THERE ARE NO OTHER KINDS OF TACOS!!

If you have time, become king of the chainsaw crabs while you're there.

HAIL!

HAIL!

Then get as many meatballs as you can carry.

Now that you've got your meatballs, you'll be ready to make those delicious meatball tacos!

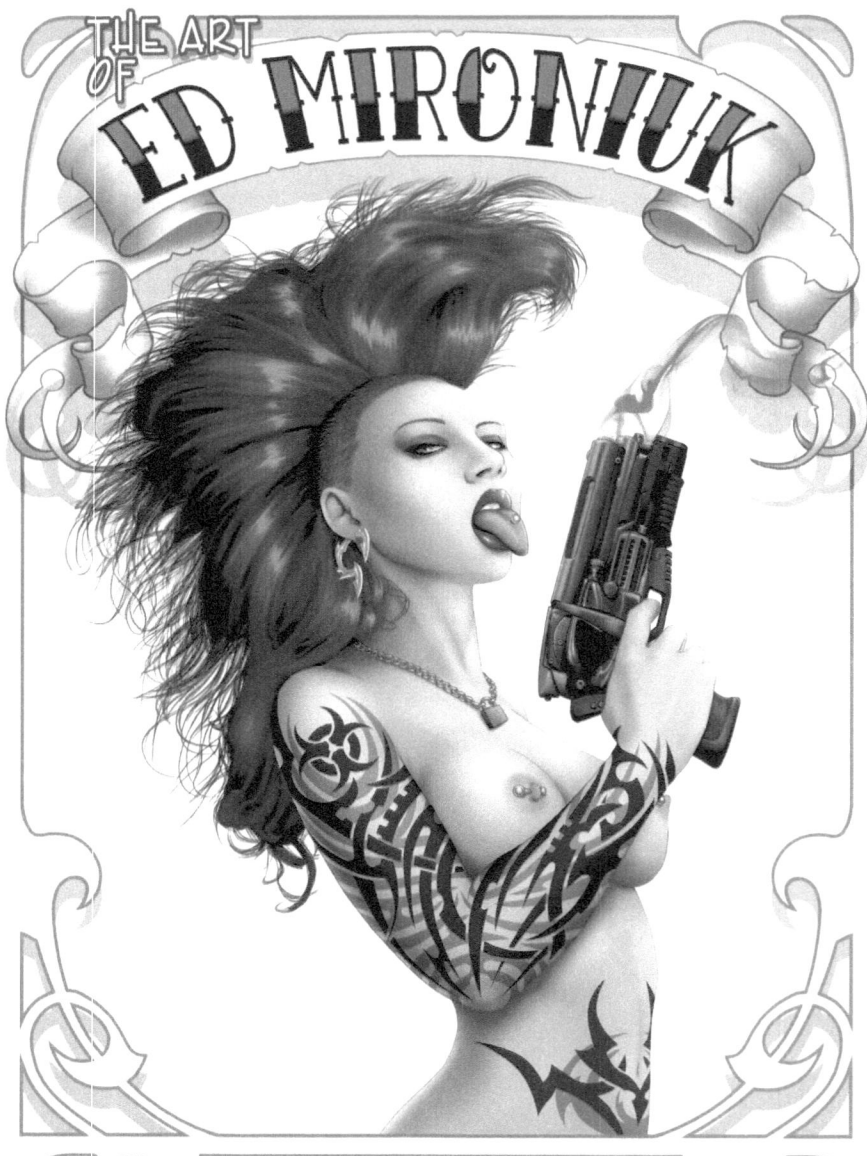

ABOUT THE AUTHOR

Carlton Mellick III is one of the leading authors of the bizarro fiction subgenre. Since 2001, his books have drawn an international cult following, despite the fact that they have been shunned by most libraries and chain bookstores.

He won the Wonderland Book Award for his novel, *Warrior Wolf Women of the Wasteland*, in 2009. His short fiction has appeared in *Vice Magazine, The Year's Best Fantasy and Horror #16, The Magazine of Bizarro Fiction,* and *Zombies: Encounters with the Hungry Dead*, among others. He is also a graduate of Clarion West, where he studied under the likes of Chuck Palahniuk, Connie Willis, and Cory Doctorow.

He lives in Portland, OR, the bizarro fiction mecca.

Visit him online at **www.carltonmellick.com**

BIZARRO BOOKS

CATALOG   SPRING 2012

ERASERHEAD PRESS

Your major resource for the bizarro fiction genre:

WWW.BIZARROCENTRAL.COM

Introduce yourselves to the bizarro fiction genre and all of its authors with the Bizarro Starter Kit series. Each volume features short novels and short stories by ten of the leading bizarro authors, designed to give you a perfect sampling of the genre for only $10.

BB-0X1
"The Bizarro Starter Kit" (Orange)
Featuring D. Harlan Wilson, Carlton Mellick III, Jeremy Robert Johnson, Kevin L Donihe, Gina Ranalli, Andre Duza, Vincent W. Sakowski, Steve Beard, John Edward Lawson, and Bruce Taylor.
236 pages $10

BB-0X2
"The Bizarro Starter Kit" (Blue)
Featuring Ray Fracalossy, Jeremy C. Shipp, Jordan Krall, Mykle Hansen, Andersen Prunty, Eckhard Gerdes, Bradley Sands, Steve Aylett, Christian TeBordo, and Tony Rauch. **244 pages $10**

BB-0X2
"The Bizarro Starter Kit" (Purple)
Featuring Russell Edson, Athena Villaverde, David Agranoff, Matthew Revert, Andrew Goldfarb, Jeff Burk, Garrett Cook, Kris Saknussemm, Cody Goodfellow, and Cameron Pierce **264 pages $10**

BB-001 "The Kafka Effekt" D. Harlan Wilson — A collection of forty-four irreal short stories loosely written in the vein of Franz Kafka, with more than a pinch of William S. Burroughs sprinkled on top. **211 pages $14**

BB-002 "Satan Burger" Carlton Mellick III — The cult novel that put Carlton Mellick III on the map ... Six punks get jobs at a fast food restaurant owned by the devil in a city violently overpopulated by surreal alien cultures. **236 pages $14**

BB-003 "Some Things Are Better Left Unplugged" Vincent Sakwoski — Join The Man and his Nemesis, the obese tabby, for a nightmare roller coaster ride into this postmodern fantasy. **152 pages $10**

BB-004 "Shall We Gather At the Garden?" Kevin L Donihe — Donihe's Debut novel. Midgets take over the world, The Church of Lionel Richie vs. The Church of the Byrds, plant porn and more! **244 pages $14**

BB-005 "Razor Wire Pubic Hair" Carlton Mellick III — A genderless humandildo is purchased by a razor dominatrix and brought into her nightmarish world of bizarre sex and mutilation. **176 pages $11**

BB-006 "Stranger on the Loose" D. Harlan Wilson — The fiction of Wilson's 2nd collection is planted in the soil of normalcy, but what grows out of that soil is a dark, witty, otherworldly jungle... **228 pages $14**

BB-007 "The Baby Jesus Butt Plug" Carlton Mellick III — Using clones of the Baby Jesus for anal sex will be the hip sex fetish of the future. **92 pages $10**

BB-008 "Fishyfleshed" Carlton Mellick III — The world of the past is an illogical flatland lacking in dimension and color, a sick-scape of crispy squid people wandering the desert for no apparent reason. **260 pages $14**

BB-009 **"Dead Bitch Army" Andre Duza** — Step into a world filled with racist teenagers, cannibals, 100 warped Uncle Sams, automobiles with razor-sharp teeth, living graffiti, and a pissed-off zombie bitch out for revenge. **344 pages $16**

BB-010 **"The Menstruating Mall" Carlton Mellick III** — "The Breakfast Club meets Chopping Mall as directed by David Lynch." - Brian Keene **212 pages $12**

BB-011 **"Angel Dust Apocalypse" Jeremy Robert Johnson** — Meth-heads, man-made monsters, and murderous Neo-Nazis. "Seriously amazing short stories..." - Chuck Palahniuk, author of Fight Club   **184 pages $11**

BB-012 **"Ocean of Lard" Kevin L Donihe / Carlton Mellick III** — A parody of those old Choose Your Own Adventure kid's books about some very odd pirates sailing on a sea made of animal fat. **176 pages $12**

BB-015 **"Foop!" Chris Genoa** — Strange happenings are going on at Dactyl, Inc, the world's first and only time travel tourism company.
"A surreal pie in the face!" - Christopher Moore   **300 pages $14**

BB-020 **"Punk Land" Carlton Mellick III** — In the punk version of Heaven, the anarchist utopia is threatened by corporate fascism and only Goblin, Mortician's sperm, and a blue-mohawked female assassin named Shark Girl can stop them. **284 pages $15**

BB-027 **"Siren Promised" Jeremy Robert Johnson & Alan M Clark** — Nominated for the Bram Stoker Award. A potent mix of bad drugs, bad dreams, brutal bad guys, and surreal/incredible art by Alan M. Clark. **190 pages $13**

BB-031**"Sea of the Patchwork Cats" Carlton Mellick III** — A quiet dreamlike tale set in the ashes of the human race. For Mellick enthusiasts who also adore The Twilight Zone. **112 pages $10**

BB-032 **"Extinction Journals" Jeremy Robert Johnson** — An uncanny voyage across a newly nuclear America where one man must confront the problems associated with loneliness, insane dieties, radiation, love, and an ever-evolving cockroach suit with a mind of its own. **104 pages $10**

BB-037 **"The Haunted Vagina" Carlton Mellick III** — It's difficult to love a woman whose vagina is a gateway to the world of the dead. **132 pages $10**

BB-043 **"War Slut" Carlton Mellick III** — Part "1984," part "Waiting for Godot," and part action horror video game adaptation of John Carpenter's "The Thing." **116 pages $10**

BB-047 **"Sausagey Santa" Carlton Mellick III** — A bizarro Christmas tale featuring Santa as a piratey mutant with a body made of sausages. 124 pages $10

BB-048 **"Misadventures in a Thumbnail Universe" Vincent Sakowski** — Dive deep into the surreal and satirical realms of neo-classical Blender Fiction, filled with television shoes and flesh-filled skies. **120 pages $10**

BB-053 **"Ballad of a Slow Poisoner" Andrew Goldfarb** — Millford Mutterwurst sat down on a Tuesday to take his afternoon tea, and made the unpleasant discovery that his elbows were becoming flatter. **128 pages $10**

BB-055 **"Help! A Bear is Eating Me" Mykle Hansen** — The bizarro, heartwarming, magical tale of poor planning, hubris and severe blood loss...
150 pages $11

BB-056 **"Piecemeal June" Jordan Krall** — A man falls in love with a living sex doll, but with love comes danger when her creator comes after her with crab-squid assassins. **90 pages $9**

BB-058 **"The Overwhelming Urge" Andersen Prunty** — A collection of bizarro tales by Andersen Prunty. **150 pages $11**

BB-059 **"Adolf in Wonderland" Carlton Mellick III** — A dreamlike adventure that takes a young descendant of Adolf Hitler's design and sends him down the rabbit hole into a world of imperfection and disorder. **180 pages $11**

BB-061 **"Ultra Fuckers" Carlton Mellick III** — Absurdist suburban horror about a couple who enter an upper middle class gated community but can't find their way out. **108 pages $9**

BB-062 **"House of Houses" Kevin L. Donihe** — An odd man wants to marry his house. Unfortunately, all of the houses in the world collapse at the same time in the Great House Holocaust. Now he must travel to House Heaven to find his departed fiancee. **172 pages $11**

BB-064 **"Squid Pulp Blues" Jordan Krall** — In these three bizarro-noir novellas, the reader is thrown into a world of murderers, drugs made from squid parts, deformed gun-toting veterans, and a mischievous apocalyptic donkey. **204 pages $12**

BB-065 **"Jack and Mr. Grin" Andersen Prunty** — "When Mr. Grin calls you can hear a smile in his voice. Not a warm and friendly smile, but the kind that seizes your spine in fear. You don't need to pay your phone bill to hear it. That smile is in every line of Prunty's prose." - Tom Bradley. **208 pages $12**

BB-066 **"Cybernetrix" Carlton Mellick III** — What would you do if your normal everyday world was slowly mutating into the video game world from Tron? **212 pages $12**

BB-072 **"Zerostrata" Andersen Prunty** — Hansel Nothing lives in a tree house, suffers from memory loss, has a very eccentric family, and falls in love with a woman who runs naked through the woods every night. **144 pages $11**

BB-073 "The Egg Man" Carlton Mellick III — It is a world where humans reproduce like insects. Children are the property of corporations, and having an enormous ten-foot brain implanted into your skull is a grotesque sexual fetish. Mellick's industrial urban dystopia is one of his darkest and grittiest to date. **184 pages $11**

BB-074 "Shark Hunting in Paradise Garden" Cameron Pierce — A group of strange humanoid religious fanatics travel back in time to the Garden of Eden to discover it is invested with hundreds of giant flying maneating sharks. **150 pages $10**

BB-075 "Apeshit" Carlton Mellick III - Friday the 13th meets Visitor Q. Six hipster teens go to a cabin in the woods inhabited by a deformed killer. An incredibly fucked-up parody of B-horror movies with a bizarro slant. **192 pages $12**

BB-076 "Fuckers of Everything on the Crazy Shitting Planet of the Vomit At smosphere" Mykle Hansen - Three bizarro satires. Monster Cocks, Journey to the Center of Agnes Cuddlebottom, and Crazy Shitting Planet. **228 pages $12**

BB-077 "The Kissing Bug" Daniel Scott Buck — In the tradition of Roald Dahl, Tim Burton, and Edward Gorey, comes this bizarro anti-war children's story about a bohemian conenose kissing bug who falls in love with a human woman. **116 pages $10**

BB-078 "MachoPoni" Lotus Rose — It's My Little Pony... *Bizarro* style! A long time ago Poniworld was split in two. On one side of the Jagged Line is the Pastel Kingdom, a magical land of music, parties, and positivity. On the other side of the Jagged Line is Dark Kingdom inhabited by an army of undead ponies. **148 pages $11**

BB-079 "The Faggiest Vampire" Carlton Mellick III — A Roald Dahl-esque children's story about two faggy vampires who partake in a mustache competition to find out which one is truly the faggiest. **104 pages $10**

BB-080 "Sky Tongues" Gina Ranalli — The autobiography of Sky Tongues, the biracial hermaphrodite actress with tongues for fingers. Follow her strange life story as she rises from freak to fame. **204 pages $12**

BB-081 "Washer Mouth" Kevin L. Donihe - A washing machine becomes human and pursues his dream of meeting his favorite soap opera star. **244 pages $11**

BB-082 "Shatnerquake" Jeff Burk - All of the characters ever played by William Shatner are suddenly sucked into our world. Their mission: hunt down and destroy the real William Shatner. **100 pages $10**

BB-083 "The Cannibals of Candyland" Carlton Mellick III - There exists a race of cannibals that are made of candy. They live in an underground world made out of candy. One man has dedicated his life to killing them all. **170 pages $11**

BB-084 "Slub Glub in the Weird World of the Weeping Willows" Andrew Goldfarb - The charming tale of a blue glob named Slub Glub who helps the weeping willows whose tears are flooding the earth. There are also Hyenas, ghosts, and a voodoo priest **100 pages $10**

BB-085 "Super Fetus" Adam Pepper - Try to abort this fetus and he'll kick your ass! **104 pages $10**

BB-086 "Fistful of Feet" Jordan Krall - A bizarro tribute to spaghetti westerns, featuring Cthulhu-worshipping Indians, a woman with four feet, a crazed gunman who is obsessed with sucking on candy, Syphilis-ridden mutants, sexually transmitted tattoos, and a house devoted to the freakiest fetishes. **228 pages $12**

BB-087 "Ass Goblins of Auschwitz" Cameron Pierce - It's Monty Python meets Nazi exploitation in a surreal nightmare as can only be imagined by Bizarro author Cameron Pierce. **104 pages $10**

BB-088 "Silent Weapons for Quiet Wars" Cody Goodfellow - "This is high-end psychological surrealist horror meets bottom-feeding low-life crime in a techno-thrilling science fiction world full of Lovecraft and magic..." -John Skipp **212 pages $12**

BB-089 "Warrior Wolf Women of the Wasteland" Carlton Mellick III
— Road Warrior Werewolves versus McDonaldland Mutants...post-apocalyptic fiction has never been quite like this. **316 pages $13**

BB-091 "Super Giant Monster Time" Jeff Burk — A tribute to choose your own adventures and Godzilla movies. Will you escape the giant monsters that are rampaging the fuck out of your city and shit? Or will you join the mob of alien-controlled punk rockers causing chaos in the streets? What happens next depends on you. **188 pages $12**

BB-092 "Perfect Union" Cody Goodfellow — "Cronenberg's THE FLY on a grand scale: human/insect gene-spliced body horror, where the human hive politics are as shocking as the gore." -John Skipp. **272 pages $13**

BB-093 "Sunset with a Beard" Carlton Mellick III — 14 stories of surreal science fiction. **200 pages $12**

BB-094 "My Fake War" Andersen Prunty — The absurd tale of an unlikely soldier forced to fight a war that, quite possibly, does not exist. It's Rambo meets Waiting for Godot in this subversive satire of American values and the scope of the human imagination. **128 pages $11**

BB-095 "Lost in Cat Brain Land" Cameron Pierce — Sad stories from a surreal world. A fascist mustache, the ghost of Franz Kafka, a desert inside a dead cat. Primordial entities mourn the death of their child. The desperate serve tea to mysterious creatures. A hopeless romantic falls in love with a pterodactyl. And much more. **152 pages $11**

BB-096 "The Kobold Wizard's Dildo of Enlightenment +2" Carlton Mellick III — A Dungeons and Dragons parody about a group of people who learn they are only made up characters in an AD&D campaign and must find a way to resist their nerdy teenaged players and retarded dungeon master in order to survive. **232 pages $12**

BB-098 "A Hundred Horrible Sorrows of Ogner Stump" Andrew Goldfarb — Goldfarb's acclaimed comic series. A magical and weird journey into the horrors of everyday life. **164 pages $11**

BB-099 **"Pickled Apocalypse of Pancake Island" Cameron Pierce**—A demented fairy tale about a pickle, a pancake, and the apocalypse. **102 pages $8**

BB-100 **"Slag Attack" Andersen Prunty**— Slag Attack features four visceral, noir stories about the living, crawling apocalypse.A slag is what survivors are calling the slug-like maggots raining from the sky, burrowing inside people, and hollowing out their flesh and their sanity. **148 pages $11**

BB-101 **"Slaughterhouse High" Robert Devereaux**—A place where schools are built with secret passageways, rebellious teens get zippers installed in their mouths and genitals, and once a year, on that special night, one couple is slaughtered and the bits of their bodies are kept as souvenirs. **304 pages $13**

BB-102 **"The Emerald Burrito of Oz" John Skipp & Marc Levinthal** —OZ IS REAL! Magic is real! The gate is really in Kansas! And America is finally allowing Earth tourists to visit this weird-ass, mysterious land. But when Gene of Los Angeles heads off for summer vacation in the Emerald City, little does he know that a war is brewing...a war that could destroy both worlds. **280 pages $13**

BB-103 **"The Vegan Revolution... with Zombies" David Agranoff** — When there's no more meat in hell, the vegans will walk the earth. **160 pages $11**

BB-104 **"The Flappy Parts" Kevin L Donihe**—Poems about bunnies, LSD, and police abuse. You know, things that matter. 132 **pages $11**

BB-105 **"Sorry I Ruined Your Orgy" Bradley Sands**—Bizarro humorist Bradley Sands returns with one of the strangest, most hilarious collections of the year. **130 pages $11**

BB-106 **"Mr. Magic Realism" Bruce Taylor**—Like Golden Age science fiction comics written by Freud, *Mr. Magic Realism* is a strange, insightful adventure that spans the furthest reaches of the galaxy, exploring the hidden caverns in the hearts and minds of men, women, aliens, and biomechanical cats. **152 pages $11**

BB-107 **"Zombies and Shit" Carlton Mellick III**—"Battle Royale" meets "Return of the Living Dead." Mellick's bizarro tribute to the zombie genre. **308 pages $13**

BB-108 **"The Cannibal's Guide to Ethical Living" Mykle Hansen**— Over a five star French meal of fine wine, organic vegetables and human flesh, a lunatic delivers a witty, chilling, disturbingly sane argument in favor of eating the rich.. **184 pages $11**

BB-109 **"Starfish Girl" Athena Villaverde**—In a post-apocalyptic underwater dome society, a girl with a starfish growing from her head and an assassin with sea anenome hair are on the run from a gang of mutant fish men. **160 pages $11**

BB-110 **"Lick Your Neighbor" Chris Genoa**—Mutant ninjas, a talking whale, kung fu masters, maniacal pilgrims, and an alcoholic clown populate Chris Genoa's surreal, darkly comical and unnerving reimagining of the first Thanksgiving. **303 pages $13**

BB-111 **"Night of the Assholes" Kevin L. Donihe**—A plague of assholes is infecting the countryside. Normal everyday people are transforming into jerks, snobs, dicks, and douchebags. And they all have only one purpose: to make your life a living hell.. **192 pages $11**

BB-112 **"Jimmy Plush, Teddy Bear Detective" Garrett Cook**—Hard-boiled cases of a private detective trapped within a teddy bear body. **180 pages $11**

BB-113 **"The Deadheart Shelters" Forrest Armstrong**—The hip hop lovechild of William Burroughs and Dali... **144 pages $11**

BB-114 **"Eyeballs Growing All Over Me... Again" Tony Raugh**— Absurd, surreal, playful, dream-like, whimsical, and a lot of fun to read. **144 pages $11**

BB-115 **"Whargoul" Dave Brockie** — From the killing grounds of Stalingrad to the death camps of the holocaust. From torture chambers in Iraq to race riots in the United States, the Whargoul was there, killing and raping. **244 pages $12**

BB-116 **"By the Time We Leave Here, We'll Be Friends" J. David Osborne** — A David Lynchian nightmare set in a Russian gulag, where its prisoners, guards, traitors, soldiers, lovers, and demons fight for survival and their own rapidly deteriorating humanity. **168 pages $11**

BB-117 **"Christmas on Crack" edited by Carlton Mellick III** — Perverted Christmas Tales for the whole family! . . . as long as every member of your family is over the age of 18. **168 pages $11**

BB-118 **"Crab Town" Carlton Mellick III** — Radiation fetishists, balloon people, mutant crabs, sail-bike road warriors, and a love affair between a woman and an H-Bomb. This is one mean asshole of a city. Welcome to Crab Town. **100 pages $8**

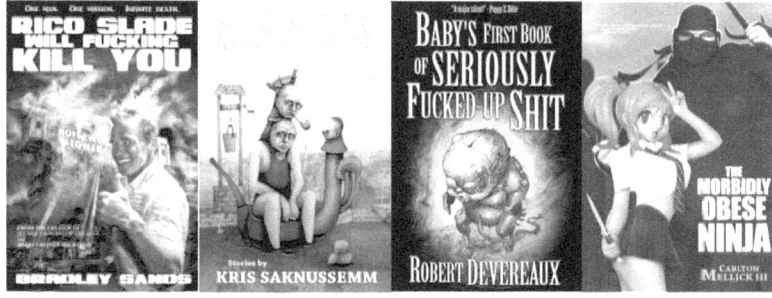

BB-119 **"Rico Slade Will Fucking Kill You" Bradley Sands** — Rico Slade is an action hero. Rico Slade can rip out a throat with his bare hands. Rico Slade's favorite food is the honey-roasted peanut. Rico Slade will fucking kill everyone. A novel. **122 pages $8**

BB-120 **"Sinister Miniatures" Kris Saknussemm** — The definitive collection of short fiction by Kris Saknussemm, confirming that he is one of the best, most daring writers of the weird to emerge in the twenty-first century. **180 pages $11**

BB-121 **"Baby's First Book of Seriously Fucked up Shit" Robert Devereaux** — Ten stories of the strange, the gross, and the just plain fucked up from one of the most original voices in horror. **176 pages $11**

BB-122 **"The Morbidly Obese Ninja" Carlton Mellick III** — These days, if you want to run a successful company . . . you're going to need a lot of ninjas. **92 pages $8**

BB-123 **"Abortion Arcade" Cameron Pierce** — An intoxicating blend of body horror and midnight movie madness, reminiscent of early David Lynch and the splatterpunks at their most sublime. **172 pages $11**

BB-124 **"Black Hole Blues" Patrick Wensink** — A hilarious double helix of country music and physics. **196 pages $11**

BB-125 **"Barbarian Beast Bitches of the Badlands" Carlton Mellick III** — Three prequels and sequels to *Warrior Wolf Women of the Wasteland.* **284 pages $13**

BB-126 **"The Traveling Dildo Salesman" Kevin L. Donihe** — A nightmare comedy about destiny, faith, and sex toys. Also featuring Donihe's most lurid and infamous short stories: *Milky Agitation, Two-Way Santa, The Helen Mower, Living Room Zombies,* and *Revenge of the Living Masturbation Rag.* **108 pages $8**

BB-127 **"Metamorphosis Blues" Bruce Taylor** — Enter a land of love beasts, intergalactic cowboys, and rock 'n roll. A land where Sears Catalogs are doorways to insanity and men keep mysterious black boxes. Welcome to the monstrous mind of Mr. Magic Realism. **136 pages $11**

BB-128 **"The Driver's Guide to Hitting Pedestrians" Andersen Prunty** — A pocket guide to the twenty-three most painful things in life, written by the most well-adjusted man in the universe. **108 pages $8**

BB-129 **"Island of the Super People" Kevin Shamel** — Four students and their anthropology professor journey to a remote island to study its indigenous population. But this is no ordinary native culture. They're super heroes and villains with flesh costumes and outlandish abilities like self-detonation, musical eyelashes, and microwave hands. **194 pages $11**

BB-130 **"Fantastic Orgy" Carlton Mellick III** — Shark Sex, mutant cats, and strange sexually transmitted diseases. Featuring the stories: *Candy-coated, Ear Cat, Fantastic Orgy, City Hobgoblins,* and *Porno in August.* **136 pages $9**

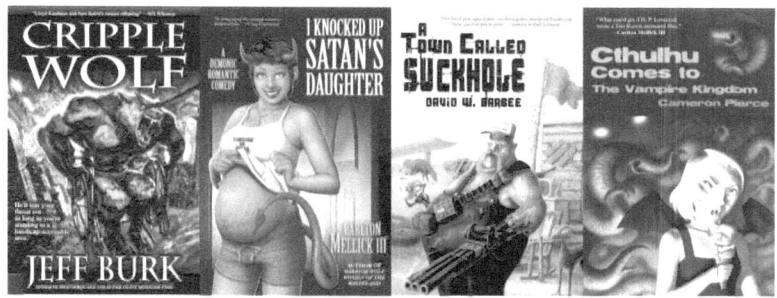

BB-131 **"Cripple Wolf" Jeff Burk** — Part man. Part wolf. 100% crippled. Also including *Punk Rock Nursing Home, Adrift with Space Badgers, Cook for Your Life, Just Another Day in the Park, Frosty and the Full Monty*, and *House of Cats.* **152 pages $10**

BB-132 **"I Knocked Up Satan's Daughter" Carlton Mellick III** — An adorable, violent, fantastical love story. A romantic comedy for the bizarro fiction reader. **152 pages $10**

BB-133 **"A Town Called Suckhole" David W. Barbee** — Far into the future, in the nuclear bowels of post-apocalyptic Dixie, there is a town. A town of derelict mobile homes, ancient junk, and mutant wildlife. A town of slack jawed rednecks who bask in the splendors of moonshine and mud boggin'. A town dedicated to the bloody and demented legacy of the Old South. A town called Suckhole. **144 pages $10**

BB-134 **"Cthulhu Comes to the Vampire Kingdom" Cameron Pierce** — What you'd get if H. P. Lovecraft wrote a Tim Burton animated film. **148 pages $11**

BB-135 **"I am Genghis Cum" Violet LeVoit** — From the savage Arctic tundra to post-partum mutations to your missing daughter's unmarked grave, join visionary madwoman Violet LeVoit in this non-stop eight-story onslaught of full-tilt Bizarro punk lit thrills. **124 pages $9**

BB-136 **"Haunt" Laura Lee Bahr** — A tripping-balls Los Angeles noir, where a mysterious dame drags you through a time-warping Bizarro hall of mirrors. **316 pages $13**

BB-137 **"Amazing Stories of the Flying Spaghetti Monster" edited by Cameron Pierce** — Like an all-spaghetti evening of Adult Swim, the Flying Spaghetti Monster will show you the many realms of His Noodly Appendage. Learn of those who worship him and the lives he touches in distant, mysterious ways. **228 pages $12**

BB-138 **"Wave of Mutilation" Douglas Lain** — A dream-pop exploration of modern architecture and the American identity, *Wave of Mutilation* is a Zen finger trap for the 21st century. **100 pages $8**

BB-139 **"Hooray for Death!" Mykle Hansen** — Famous Author Mykle Hansen draws unconventional humor from deaths tiny and large, and invites you to laugh while you can. **128 pages $10**

BB-140 **"Hypno-hog's Moonshine Monster Jamboree" Andrew Goldfarb** — Hicks, Hogs, Horror! Goldfarb is back with another strange illustrated tale of backwoods weirdness. **120 pages $9**

BB-141 **"Broken Piano For President" Patrick Wensink** — A comic masterpiece about the fast food industry, booze, and the necessity to choose happiness over work and security. **372 pages $15**

BB-142 **"Please Do Not Shoot Me in the Face" Bradley Sands** — A novel in three parts, *Please Do Not Shoot Me in the Face: A Novel*, is the story of one boy detective, the worst ninja in the world, and the great American fast food wars. It is a novel of loss, destruction, and--incredibly--genuine hope. **224 pages $12**

BB-143 **"Santa Steps Out" Robert Devereaux** — Sex, Death, and Santa Claus ... The ultimate erotic Christmas story is back. **294 pages $13**

BB-144 **"Santa Conquers the Homophobes" Robert Devereaux** — "I wish I could hope to ever attain one-thousandth the perversity of Robert Devereaux's toenail clippings." - Poppy Z. Brite **316 pages $13**

BB-145 **"We Live Inside You" Jeremy Robert Johnson** — "Jeremy Robert Johnson is dancing to a way different drummer. He loves language, he loves the edge, and he loves us people. These stories have range and style and wit. This is entertainment... and literature."- Jack Ketchum **188 pages $11**

BB-146 **"Clockwork Girl" Athena Villaverde** — Urban fairy tales for the weird girl in all of us. Like a combination of Francesca Lia Block, Charles de Lint, Kathe Koja, Tim Burton, and Hayao Miyazaki, her stories are cute, kinky, edgy, magical, provocative, and strange, full of poetic imagery and vicious sexuality. **160 pages $10**

BB-147 **"Armadillo Fists" Carlton Mellick III** — A weird-as-hell gangster story set in a world where people drive giant mechanical dinosaurs instead of cars. **168 pages $11**

BB-148 **"Gargoyle Girls of Spider Island" Cameron Pierce** — Four college seniors venture out into open waters for the tropical party weekend of a lifetime. Instead of a teenage sex fantasy, they find themselves in a nightmare of pirates, sharks, and sex-crazed monsters. **100 pages $8**

BB-149 **"The Handsome Squirm" by Carlton Mellick III** — Like Franz Kafka's *The Trial* meets an erotic body horror version of *The Blob*. **158 pages $11**

BB-150 **"Tentacle Death Trip" Jordan Krall** — It's *Death Race 2000* meets H. P. Lovecraft in bizarro author Jordan Krall's best and most suspenseful work to date. **224 pages $12**

BB-151 **"The Obese" Nick Antosca** — Like Alfred Hitchcock's *The Birds*... but with obese people. **108 pages $10**

BB-152 **"All-Monster Action!" Cody Goodfellow** — The world gave him a blank check and a demand: Create giant monsters to fight our wars. But Dr. Otaku was not satisfied with mere chaos and mass destruction.... **216 pages $12**

BB-153 **"Ugly Heaven" Carlton Mellick III** — Heaven is no longer a paradise. It was once a blissful utopia full of wonders far beyond human comprehension. But the afterlife is now in ruins. It has become an ugly, lonely wasteland populated by strange monstrous beasts, masturbating angels, and sad man-like beings wallowing in the remains of the once-great Kingdom of God. **106 pages $8**

BB-154 **"Space Walrus" Kevin L. Donihe** — Walter is supposed to go where no walrus has ever gone before, but all this astronaut walrus really wants is to take it easy on the intense training, escape the chimpanzee bullies, and win the love of his human trainer Dr. Stephanie. **160 pages $11**

www.ingramcontent.com/pod-product-compliance
Lightning Source LLC
Chambersburg PA
CBHW020342260626
47156CB00004B/1646